MAN UP

Stephanie Perry Moore
& Derrick Moore

SADDLEBACK
PUBLISHING

FRESH GUY

Truly Fine

Deep Soul

Quiet Strength

Stand Firm

Man Up

SADDLEBACK
PUBLISHING
www.sdlback.com

Copyright © 2014 by Saddleback Educational Publishing
All rights reserved. No part of this book may be reproduced in any form or
by any means, electronic or mechanical, including photocopying, recording,
scanning, or by any information storage and retrieval system, without the written
permission of the publisher. SADDLEBACK EDUCATIONAL PUBLISHING
and any associated logos are trademarks and/or registered trademarks of
Saddleback Educational Publishing.

ISBN-13: 978-1-62250-687-3
ISBN-10: 1-62250-687-1
eBook: 978-1-61247-752-7

Printed in Guangzhou, China
NOR/1213/CA21302311

18 17 16 15 14   1 2 3 4 5

To Vad Lee

It's your time to lead, both on and off the football field. We know you will be a difference maker. Thank you for your support of the Tech Chaplaincy Program. We are grateful for your heart and your desire to do what's right. Remember as you take each step that you are the man. We pray that you remain upbeat and believe that all you dream of will be yours. May every reader work as hard as you do.

You are a young man we are proud to know … peace and love!

ACKNOWLEDGEMENTS

No doubt life can be tough. Peer pressure, gang violence, economic worries, cultural differences, parent problems, self-esteem issues, and other woes can weigh heavy on your heart. Worst of all is when you make mistakes that really bring you down. You must find a way to get out of your own way.

Well, though stress can be real, it does not have to keep you bummed out. Learn from your circumstances and decide to make your life better. Stand up against what's wrong in your world and do what is right. Help others and care about yourself. Work on your weaknesses and continue developing your strengths. Study hard, work hard, and play hard ... just don't mix them. The point of this book is leave the foolishness behind. Be a good friend. Be a true gentleman, and be a difference maker. Man up!

Here is a big thank you to all those who help us step up our writing game.

Acknowledgements

To our parents, Dr. Franklin and Shirley Perry Sr. and Ann Redding, because you stand up in every area of your life, we can man up and be responsible too.

To our publisher, especially the Saddleback Publishing office staff, because you made sure we were well-taken care of all along this series' writing journey, we manned up and got the books in.

To our extended family: brothers, Dennis Perry and Victor Moore, sister, Sherry Moore, godparents, Walter and Marjorie Kimbrough, Jim and Deen Sanders, young nephews, Franklin Perry III, Kadarius Moore, and godsons, Danton Lynn, Dakari Jones, and Dorian Lee, because you bless our lives, we can man up and bless others.

To our assistants: Candace Johnson, Shaneen Clay, and Alyxandra Pinkston, because you juggled so much and worked tirelessly to help us get this book in, we manned up and did our part.

To our friends who mean so much: Paul and Susan Johnson, Chan and Laurie Gailey, Antonio and Gloria London, Chett and Lakeba Williams, Jay and Deborah Spencer, Bobby and Sarah Lundy, Harry and Torian Colon, Byron and Kim Forest, Chris and Jenell Clark, Donald and Deborah Bradley, because of your great friendship, we can man up and show others how to be good friends also.

To our teens: Dustyn, who just graduated from high school; Sydni, who won the girls' golf tournament for our county; and Sheldyn, who successfully finished her first year of high school, because you are holding your own, we strive to man up and be better parents.

To the media specialists, school administrators, teachers, and educational companies across the country that support us, especially the folks in Cobb County that I haven't met yet, because all you do in your great school system (especially at Hillgrove High) moved us, we manned up and wrote about Grovehill High.

To our readers, who we pray will thrive at reading, because you are on book five of the Grovehill Giants series, we manned up and wrote a fifth book that you could read.

And to our Savior, who manned up and hung on the cross, we can man up and stick with this life until we are with you.

Why Me?

My girlfriend, Yaris Fernandez, and I had finally crossed the intimacy threshold. She held me off for a while, wanting to stay a good girl, but I convinced her that my love was real. When she finally trusted me, we were able to share something special. Once we started, we couldn't stop. For the last few weeks, every day we found a way to be together. There was nothing I liked more, and I actually wished I was on my way to be with her now.

Instead, I was on a bus with my teammates heading to the first Grovehill Giants playoff game of my junior year. We weren't getting to host it because we lost some games along the stretch, but we were still in it. With the talent we had, we planned to take it all the way to the Dome for a chance to win the state title. Scouts were coming, so this was put-up or shut-up time. The quarterback spot was questionable, though, because we all felt that our coach should be playing this senior, Chaz O'Neal, instead of this junior big-mouthed jerk named Gage whose daddy helped him secure the spot. But it was what it was. Coach wasn't changing it, and as long as I showed up and did my part as the kickoff return man and strong safety, we'd be okay.

I had had a great season. I ran four kickoffs back for touchdowns—one of them ninety-nine yards—and I had seven interceptions. I wanted more, but Coach said I was leading our region and he was satisfied. However, I figured this was my chance to get more, so I was going to be more aggressive so that I could be one of the reasons, if not the full reason, why we won.

"All right, boys, y'all need to come on and get off of that bus," Coach Swords said as he stepped onto the bus I was on. "You guys are moving mighty slow. I hope this isn't any indication of how y'all are planning to perform today. These guys down here in Middle Georgia don't play. Y'all got to be on your A game. Chop, chop!"

And so we started moving faster, but Coach couldn't blame us if it was taking a minute to get the lead out. The bus ride had given us a couple of hours to chill, contemplate life, think about the game ahead, and rest up. As a team we were tired since most of us were knocked out. For a few of us, however, our adrenaline was flowing. We knew it was our time, and when my boy Ryder, who was arguably the best linebacker in the state, patted me on the back and said, "All right! Let's go!" I got even more hyped.

In the locker room, I could tell most of us were nervous. We were up for the challenge, but the Ridgeland Raiders were the number-one seed. That meant they were supposed to go all the way. We'd barely gotten in the playoffs. We knew we were better than our ranking, but these guys were studs. It almost felt like the Raiders were already a Division I team or something. They were fast, strong, and skilled. They had a crowd that was rowdy and ready to tear into us. We played them during the regular season, and it wasn't any fun. They gave us our first loss, and though it wasn't a butt whupping, at the end of the day, if you lose, what does it matter? None of us wanted to take that long ride home again feeling the way we did back at the start of the season.

Before we took the field to warm up, Coach called us all around him and said, "Listen, I said it all year: we're not Giants for no reason. They might appear like they have the edge because of home-field advantage. They might be a little bigger. And sure, they're ranked higher, and their record's better. But so what? They don't have your heart!

"You guys all need to get rid of the butterflies right now. You're not cheerleaders; you're football players here to win a game and take care of business, so go ahead and man up. Think about what you got to do today; don't worry about your teammates. Stay in your lane, take care of your responsibilities, and if everyone plays at his highest level, the best he can, giving all he's got, we will win! Giants on three." We all put our hands in. He said, "One, two, three ..."

We all yelled, "Giants!"

When we ran out on the field to warm up, Ryder was on one side of me, and Ford was on the other. Ford was a running back. Our friend Stone—a tight end—was jogging out to meet us. Our other friend Emerson was a kicker, and boy was he good. He was so quiet that you'd never know he was such a football star until you saw him kick. They were my boys.

Ryder joked to Ford, "Coach Swords got him some balls now!"

"What you talking about, man?" Ford said.

"I don't know, but your mama must be doing something right because he's coming into his own. Giving that cool speech, trying to get us all ready, talking like a man ..."

"Ha-ha-ha," Ford said, definitely not happy with what Ryder was insinuating, but everyone knew it was true.

At the beginning of the season, Coach Swords had been a little timid—he couldn't walk and chew bubble gum at the same time. I mean, he was never a bad coach, but he just wasn't as forceful and as sure of himself as he was now, further down the stretch, since he'd started dating Ford's mother. And at first Ford hated it, and it looked like he still hated being teased about it, but honestly, I'd have given anything to have Coach Swords as my mentor and father figure.

One thing Ford and I had in common was that our biological fathers weren't living in the house. I wasn't sure of everything in Ford's situation. I knew his dad lived in Tennessee; we all lived in Cobb County, Georgia. My dad had left for New York, but he was still giving my mom some problems. She wasn't telling me everything that they were dealing with, but I knew he was being a jerk. At sixteen, nearing seventeen, I wished that I had a dad to bounce things off of. That wasn't happening.

About thirty minutes later, we came back out on the field. Their crazy fans were intimidating. They were calling us names, and some were even threatening our lives. When someone threw a can at my helmet, I got stressed.

They won the toss and selected to defer to the second half, which meant they were kicking the ball off to us, and we had to go against the wind. All of their players looked like giants. When the ball came flying in my direction, I thought I could get it for a fair catch. But a gust of wind knocked it off course, and because those jokers were coming down the field so fast, nerves got the best of me, and I bobbled it. They got the ball on our ten-yard line, and everybody on my team was livid at me. How do you come off the sidelines knowing that they are about to get a touchdown, and it's your freaking fault?

"Get on back out there!" Coach Swords said. "Defend it; they're going to throw it in the corner!"

But at ten yards out, I thought for sure they'd run it, so I didn't play my man close. And wouldn't you know it, on the very first play they tossed it up in the corner of the end zone where I should have been defending, and they got a touchdown just like that. If I thought my teammates were pissed before, then I had no clue what being upset was. Why'd I have to be the one to get us off to a bad start? As the game progressed, I couldn't get my confidence back. Why'd I have to be the one who kept making mistakes?

I played horribly. The first playoff game I was starting, and I messed up every play I was involved in. I really had no explanation for it. It wasn't like I was unprepared. I wasn't injured. I just couldn't keep it together. My instincts were off, and now my team would not have a chance at the state title because of me. I'd started the game with hopes of an MVP trophy; by the end of it, if they awarded a least valuable player award, it would have gone to me.

When the game was over, we had to line up to head midfield and shake the other players' hands. I really wasn't in the mood. Sportsman-ship dictated it, though.

Gage just happened to be behind me, or maybe he was purposefully there because he wouldn't shut his big mouth. "You talked all this junk all year about how I shouldn't be the quarterback, how we needed somebody else, how my arm was wack, blah, blah, blah. No matter how bad you think I played all year, your perfor-mance today was way worse. You're a chump."

"Just shut up, man," I heard Ryder say from behind Gage.

A part of me wanted to say, "It's all right. He's just telling the truth. We all know it." But I was too wounded to speak. I didn't even want to be out on the turf telling the other players good game. I gave them the game, and I had no idea how I was going to live this down.

"Man, don't worry about him," Emerson said, looking over his shoulder.

I didn't even realize Emerson was in front of me. As good as he was at kicking, because I played so bad, his three points couldn't even help close the margin to give us a chance to be competitive in the game. From start to finish, we were behind, and it was my fault. I didn't know any of the players from Ridgeland, and to me they all looked like beasts. I knew over the off-season and summer I was going to have to get more confidence, swagger, and size if I wanted to compete on the next level.

As I walked down the line and touched the Ridgeland players' hands, I realized that I was fine, and my opponents about matched up with me. But if I let myself start dwelling on how tall they were, how big they were, or how good the scouts deemed them to be, then I got intimidated. Going through the motions saying "Good game, good game, good game," I touched the last player's hand, and he grabbed mine and jerked me toward him.

His funky breath in my face, he said, "You're that safety. Thank goodness you weren't strong today. You were weak, safety. Better bring your game next time, player, because you got played."

I wasn't a punk, so no way was I going to take that. I shoved his tail, and he shoved me back even harder. Emerson and Ryder backed me up when his teammates joined in and threatened to cause a big ruckus.

"Y'all won. Go settle down somewhere," Ryder shouted to them.

Emerson said, "Come on, Hagen, man. They ain't even worth it."

"Yeah, but he was telling the truth," Gage put in, though no one even asked him.

I wanted to punch him. Or did I want to beat myself up? I took off my helmet and threw it near a bleacher. It almost hit our coach.

He rushed over to me, grabbed me by my shoulder pads, and said, "Look, you need to settle down, Cruz. All this testosterone you're displaying now—throwing your equipment, wanting to fight the other team, acting all tough—that's what I needed to see on the field today!"

"I tried, Coach, I tried. What you want me to say?" I uttered, truly dejected.

"I want you to reflect on it because the game is over, and all this attitude you're giving isn't necessary. Get yourself together and come on in this locker room so we can change and go home. Can you do that, son?"

I said nothing.

"Can you do that?" he asked again.

"Yes, sir," I said.

He let go of my shoulder pads, and I was even more ticked. If I were two, I would have lain face down on the ground and thrown a major tantrum. But I was sixteen, and the only thing I could do was figure it all out and get better next time. Problem was, for a lot of the seniors on the team, there wasn't going to be a next time. I glanced over at my teammates and saw that a lot of them looked angry.

Ryder touched my shoulder pad and said, "Everybody has a bad game every now and then."

"Yeah, man, but I didn't want to let y'all down like that in the biggest game we played."

"I know you didn't … Looks like there's a cheerleader over there who wants to say something to you. Go get your smooch on before we get on the bus. We'll talk in a minute, all right?"

"Whatever," I said, trying to hold back the water from shooting down my cheeks.

Last thing I wanted was for my girl to see me crying. Yaris was gorgeous; she looked like a mix of Kim Kardashian and Jennifer Lopez. Both of those ladies were fine, but neither one of them could hold a candle to my girl. I'd liked her for a while, but I wasn't bold enough to make a move until the start of the school year. Ever since then, we'd been tighter than tight. I could do no wrong in her eyes, but Yaris wasn't an idiot about football. I played wrong the whole game, and though she looked so sad, like she wanted to try and cheer me up, what could she say when it was my fault?

"I know I did bad," I told her.

Actually it was even harder for me to face her, so I was happy when one of the other coaches yelled that it was time to go. But Yaris didn't want to leave. I tried to stem the sulking and step up to face her.

I said, "I'm sorry, babe, you ain't got to hold your tongue. I see there's something you want to say to me. I know I did bad."

"You're not the only one on this team, Hagen. Every time the Raiders got a touchdown, we had an opportunity to get the ball back, but Gage was three and out."

She was right; our offense didn't do a lot. But I didn't give them the best field position either.

"And on one of the runs that the team had, he went right by Ryder," she continued.

"One busted play isn't the end of the world, but I had a bunch of them. Ugh, forget it," I said, not wanting to get upset at her but not wanting her to make excuses for me either.

When I got on the bus, I heard some boos. Part of me wanted to find the parties responsible and punch them in their mouths so they would shut the heck up. However, the realistic side of me thought, "If the shoe was on the other foot and somebody else messed up so bad that we didn't have a chance at winning, I'd boo his tail too." So I sat in the same seat I'd ridden down in and tried to block out all the talk around me about how pitiful I was.

Ryder leaned up and said, "Hey, man. We're just juniors. Don't sweat this. I messed up too."

"If I play like I did today next year, then I don't need to be playing," I said, truly evaluating my performance. "I just don't understand why I messed up like that."

Almost two hours later when we were pulling up at our school, I heard the rumble of motorcycle engines from across the street. I did a double take when I saw it was the Bones, a local gang that had made my life miserable. Its leader, this thug named Loco, was supposed to be in jail. But there he was, sitting on one of the bikes, looking menacing. Ryder saw them too.

"You're just going to get in the car and go, man."

"I thought he was locked up," I said, frustrated that if it wasn't one thing, it was another.

Why did it always have to be something? But I was going to have to man up. I couldn't run from this.

"I told y'all I wasn't going," I said to Emerson and Stone when they showed up at my house early Saturday morning.

I understood that they wanted to drive to Columbus, Georgia, to watch the girls compete for a state competition cheerleading title. But with the game I'd just had and the shock of seeing Loco out of jail, I didn't want to do anything but stay in bed all day. Problem was, my boys weren't gonna let me.

"No, no, no, we going down to see the girls, and you're coming with us," Stone said.

"Please! Ford and Ryder talked a good game, but I don't see them with y'all. Besides, all of us can't fit in your car. We're too big to be five deep in a coupe!" I said to Stone.

"For your information," Emerson said, "we're meeting the two of them at the Cracker Barrel right off the interstate."

"Look, guys, I had a horrible night last night. I just need to stay. Yaris will understand."

Stone put a hand on my shoulder and said, "What girl would understand her man not being there when everybody else got a guy there to support them? She'll be so upset that you'll never live it down. Just think about it because you know they're slated to win, and when they do, we will all be there, arms open wide, ready to give kisses, hugs, and all that good stuff. You want Yaris to be standing there looking around, wondering where you are? What you want us to tell her? Because you're a sore loser, you couldn't come support her? Man, that don't sound right. Get your stuff, and let's go."

I mean, what could I say to that? That didn't sound right, and I didn't want to leave my girl hanging like that. I cared about her way too much. I didn't use the *L* word a bunch, but I really couldn't imagine my life without her.

Twenty minutes later we were on the road. It took us about fifteen minutes to get to Cracker Barrel, where we met Ryder and Ford and got some grub. As football players, we needed to get a hearty breakfast before traveling more than one hundred miles to Columbus.

At breakfast, I really didn't want to talk about much. Ryder could go a little too far sometimes. He was my boy, but I didn't always find everything he said to be funny.

Ryder teased, "I didn't think they were going to be able to get you out the house."

"Don't start, man," Stone said to him.

"Nah, I'm just saying, he was whining on the bus real bad yesterday. And when we saw Loco, if Hagen were water, he would have turned into a block of ice, I'm telling you," Ryder said, laughing.

Fed up, I snapped, "All right, dang!"

Ryder explained, "I'm just saying. I'm happy to see you out, 'cause as crazy as the Bones are, you don't need to be by yourself right now."

"Yeah, I think that's why they didn't mess with you yesterday," Ford added.

"They didn't mess with me yesterday because we went straight from the bus to our cars and took off," I said, setting him straight.

"Yeah, but knowing them like I do, I'm sure they could have followed us," Emerson said. "Y'all know how well I know them. They came to my dad's church, vandalized it, beat me up—"

"All right, fine! I had a hand in that!" I said, upset at the reminder that I had let a gang terrorize me and make me do things that were so out of my nature.

I reached in my wallet and pulled out a twenty. "Here's my money. I'll be at the car."

Ryder opened up his wallet and placed money on the table too. "Wait up, partner."

Too through, I said, "Please, don't call me partner."

"I was just messin' with you, dang. You ain't got to be so sensitive. I thought we were going to see the girls; I didn't think I was with one already."

"Oh, see, you always got jokes; you don't know when to lay off. You of all people know how much I've been going through."

"You're right; I was right in front of you on the bus last night, and I saw your meltdown."

"I wasn't whining, pouting, and crying."

"Uh, yes you were!" Ryder said.

"Well, I had good reason."

"And I'm just saying I'm happy you're out of the funk. That's all! I'm not trying to minimize Loco and all those guys. They're crazy, and the way they were looking at all of us, we all need to be watching our backs."

"You right, you right."

"And I got your back. While I might joke around, you know I'm serious about that."

We slapped palms and did a guy hug.

"Y'all better come on. We got to get on down there. I don't know when they go on," Ford said.

Ryder messed with him. "Yeah, because you don't want Skylar to be calling you out."

"That'd be him," Ford said as he pointed at Emerson.

We all nodded. Vanessa would be the one to go off.

"That Ariel, she's high maintenance too," Emerson said, taking a jab of his own.

"I just hope they win," I said, knowing Yaris had learned some new moves. I hoped she didn't mess up. The last thing I wanted was for her to feel like I had felt yesterday if she were to let her team down. If she did, though, I'd be there.

As the three of us followed Ford and Ryder, I leaned up and hollered at Emerson sitting in the passenger seat. "You and I straight about everything that happened at your dad's church and all, right?"

"Yeah, man. We talked about that; we've been through that."

"I know, but you brought it up today, and it just doesn't seem like you're over it."

"Well, I'm not over what happened, but I'm not mad at you for being involved. Those guys are manipulative, and if Loco's out, he's pulled some strings with some high-up folks. There will still be a trial, and with our testimonies, we just got to stick together and not be intimidated."

"Y'all need anything, just let me know. My dad's got a whole security crew," Stone offered.

"Man, I don't want nobody else involved in this," I said.

As I leaned back, I thought about my father, the one who got me in this mess in the first place. He had borrowed some money from Loco, and then he fled town without bothering to pay it back. Because my mom and I were his next of kin, we were on the hook for the debt, even though my mother and I never saw a dime of the money.

My mother worked all the time. She was an assistant manager at Walmart. She pulled her weight, my dad's weight, and it seemed like she had the weight of the world on her shoulders. I wanted to make something of my life, and football seemed like a great ticket out. My mother didn't have any money to send me to college, and my grades were just okay, so I wasn't going to receive any kind of academic scholarship.

While she made good loot legitimately, we were so in debt and had so many bills that her income barely kept us afloat. That's why I was beating myself up about my performance in the playoff game. When it was my time to shine and potentially secure a football scholarship, I blew it. I appreciated that Stone and Emerson let me drift off to sleep because I hadn't gotten much of it the night before. When they woke me up, we were at the coliseum.

"Let's go see the girls."

And that we did. Watching Yaris and the rest of the Grovehill cheerleaders perform, I was proud. My teammates and I rose to our feet and joined their parents and the other fans that came to support them, yelling with all we had. It was weird for us football players to be cheering for the girls because they were usually the ones cheering for us. But I didn't mind. Since we got there right when they were going on, I didn't get to connect with Yaris beforehand. I wanted to wink at her or blow her a kiss or something to make sure that she was smiling, but I didn't want to distract her.

Thankfully, the wishes I sent her way worked along with her skills, because she did her thing. When they were crowned champions, my boys and I couldn't wait to get to our girls to hug them and congratulate them. I was going to sneak up to Yaris and surprise her, put my hands over her eyes and kiss her neck or something, but I saw her talking to this airhead cheerleader, Jillian, who I knew to always be causing trouble. I never got the chance to say congratulations for being 5A champions. As I approached them, I heard Jillian practically shout that Yaris was pregnant. With everything else I was dealing with—messing up the playoff game, finding out Loco was out of jail, handling extra responsibilities with my dad being gone—now I was learning that I was going to be a dad myself. Why me?

CHAPTER TWO

Stay Solid

Hearing that I was about to be a father shook
me to the core. It made everything else that
I'd been going through seem like kindergarten
problems. This was big boy stuff, and I wanted
to shout out, "How in the world did this happen?
I'm not ready for a baby." Part of me wanted to
demand, "Yaris, you've got to take care of this."
However, I looked into her eyes and saw she
was even more terrified than I was. She seemed
petrified. Seeing her so fragile got to me. So, I
reached out, put my arms around her, and told
her that everything was going to be okay.

As I hugged Yaris, I could see that Jillian
looked disappointed. I hated how some people

loved seeing others miserable. I wasn't going to let her take pleasure out of Yaris's pain. When Jillian saw that I was not fuming, that I wasn't going to leave Yaris, and that there wasn't going to be a big scene, she stormed away.

"I don't know how this happened. I mean, I know how this happened, but ..."

I gave her waist a reassuring squeeze. "I got you, babe. I know this is just as much my fault."

We'd been enjoying ourselves a lot. I didn't use protection, and I knew she wasn't on birth control. That hadn't stopped me from wanting to hookup, so how could I blame her? How could I be mad at my girl? How could I make this all her fault? We were in this together, and once I let her know that, she brightened a little bit.

Having Yaris close in my arms felt so good. She was holding me tight, but I couldn't get excited because this was serious. I was going to be a dad, and as much as I was telling her things were going to be okay, I was trippin'. How could I take care of a kid when I could barely take care of myself? What would happen to Yaris's college hopes and dreams if she had to raise a child?

How could I go off to school, leaving her to manage the responsibility of having a baby alone? I wasn't a squeaky clean good boy, but I wasn't a jerk either. I cared about her.

I saw her parents walking our way. I didn't even know they were in attendance. I was especially surprised to see her dad because he was always at his restaurant, but I guess it was so early in the morning that he'd have time to get back before it got crowded.

"We got to tell them," I said to Yaris as I turned her around so she could see her folks.

Mr. Fernandez was a really cool guy. I wished my own father were more like him. Not that I was trying to take him away from Yaris or anything, but he was just what a father was supposed to be. He and I had always been able to talk, and he was a great mentor. Because he had two girls, I think he dug the fact that I played sports and gave him an outlet to talk about guy stuff. I used to go by his restaurant and just mull things over with him. But lately I'd been avoiding the restaurant because I made him a promise. I told him that I would not take my relationship with Yaris to a sexual place, and it was now hard to look him in the eyes knowing that I had, many times over, broken that promise.

"You can't say anything," she said in a panicked voice.

"We got to tell your folks," I insisted. I didn't want them to find out the way I had, with some random girl blurting it out.

I just should have listened to her because when we broke the news to them, they were livid, especially her dad. I mean, he didn't beat me down or threaten to kill me or anything, but he didn't mince words, and he reminded me of the promise I'd made him. I'd let him down in a big way. I just wasn't expecting what he said next.

"I don't want you seeing my daughter ever again. Come on, Yaris, let's go."

She didn't want to leave. He wasn't taking no for an answer. I didn't want to make a scene. I'd already caused him much grief by being the other half to the whole pregnancy equation. So I felt like it was best for me to stand down, not rock the boat, and give her father time to cool off. Maybe once he saw I wasn't planning to ditch my responsibilities, that I'd help Yaris figure this out, he'd calm down a little. And even though I didn't have a penny to my name, I already had a heart for the baby. Boy or girl, I knew I wanted to be a better father to it than my dad was for me. Mr. Fernandez needed to understand that. His daughter was in tears, but he couldn't keep me from her side for long.

Five of us had to squeeze into Stone's car for the ride back. This time I took the front seat, and Emerson got in the back with Vanessa and Victoria. Emerson had been a nerd in ninth and tenth grade. He was coming out of his shell with a vengeance. I still felt bad for having gone with the gang to vandalize his dad's church. I was happy he had forgiven me for my part in it, and I was also happy to see him coming into his own. He and Vanessa were feeling each other for real.

I could tell Vanessa's half-sister, Victoria, felt a little uncomfortable sitting beside the two of them as they were making out. I wanted to turn around and say, "Uh, y'all might want to chill with all that. Isn't one teen pregnancy in the crew enough?" Instead I coughed pointedly, and Emerson got the hint.

There was silence in the car, and I wondered what was up. But when Stone said, "Man, it's going to be okay. We're all going to be here to help you guys," I realized everybody knew my girl was carrying a child.

"Yeah, man, whatever you need, just let us know," Emerson said.

"And we're going to be there for Yaris too," Victoria added.

"I'm just glad you responded the right way," Vanessa said. "I would've hated to have to come after you."

I didn't respond or laugh. I knew she was trying to make a joke, and I knew she had Yaris's back, but none of this was funny to me. The reality that I was going to be a dad was quickly setting in, and now I was feeling physically sick. Where was I going to get money for diapers? How were we going to pay for day care? Where were we going to raise it?

My situation was a mess. I felt like I couldn't breathe. As I fumbled with my collar and rolled down the window to get air, everybody in the car could tell I was frazzled.

Stone was driving, but he put his arm on my shoulder. "Keep it together, man. You got this. It might not be ideal, but you'll be okay. Got me?"

I appreciated his reassurance. Taking a deep breath, I nodded, believing some way, somehow, I'd get through this. I felt it wasn't going to be the end of the world.

"Don't come in here slamming doors, boy," my mom shouted out to me.

As soon as Stone dropped me off, all I wanted to do was go to my room and be alone. I didn't know my mom's work schedule, but I was disappointed when I saw her car in the driveway. Perhaps I'd taken out some of my frustration by shutting the front door a little too forcefully. But my mom was on me 24/7. If she gave my dad half the hell she gave me, maybe he'd get his act together. Or maybe that was why he left.

"Mom, I wasn't trying to slam the door."

"Well, you did. I'm lying on the couch trying to get some rest before I have to go to work, and you come in here throwing your weight around."

"All right, sorry, Mom," I said, really half into it.

She must have felt bad about giving me a hard time, because she got up and nicely said, "You want something to eat, honey?"

"No, Mom. Get some rest," I told her, still agitated.

"I didn't mean to get on your case," she uttered, probably realizing she'd gotten under my skin.

"It's cool, Mom. I don't want to bother you. I'm fine."

"You're not bothering me. I want to fix you something to eat. I want us to sit down and talk a little bit before I have to go to work. I miss you. I want to know about the game yesterday. I mean, I know y'all lost, but how did you play?"

"Can we talk about this later, Mom? I know you have to get ready for work."

"I don't have to go in right now. I start in a few hours. We have plenty of time. Hagen, sit yourself on down and let me fix you something. Don't want my boy to end up as skinny as a veggie burrito."

My mom wanted to baby me, but I looked over to the corner where she kept the bills and saw they were piled high. I didn't feel like eating anything because I had an upset stomach. The reality of my life was making me sick, and I guess it was showing all over my distressed face.

Feeling a headache coming on like a storm cloud on the horizon, I started massaging my forehead. As bad as I wanted the pain to subside, it just kept getting more intense. A baby, me a dad, no money, no college degree … my future was over.

When I couldn't take it anymore, I finally put my head down on the kitchen table. Hopefully my mom would get the point that I was exhausted, sick, and tired. I thought she would leave me alone or tell me to go lie down, but she came over and lifted up my head in her hands. When my eyes weren't meeting hers, she lifted my chin even higher, so much so I thought my head was going to pop off my neck.

She said sternly, "What is going on with you? Don't tell me that it's nothing. You always want to eat. You're definitely stressed out about something. What is it? Hagen, you're scaring me."

"I didn't do good in the game, Mom. I'm the reason we lost," I said.

"Oh, baby. You may feel that way, but I'm sure you weren't the reason."

"Mom, you asked me what was wrong. Please, don't patronize me. I know how I played, and it wasn't good."

She didn't even understand the rules of football; to her, just my getting out there and knocking somebody over was doing a good job. But I knew I'd messed up, and I was tired of trying to explain it.

"Okay, so you didn't have the best game. Fine, I'll give you that," she said as she waved her hand through the air like she was sweeping that behind us. "You'll be able to play again next year, and maybe you'll go even further. I believe in you, and I raised you to not get so down that you can't pull yourself up again. There's nothing wrong with feeling bad if something happens to disappoint you, but you can't wallow around all day like a pitiful puppy dog that hasn't eaten in two weeks. Just because you had one bad game, doesn't mean your life is over."

"My life *is* over!" I declared, getting up from the table and hitting it hard.

She looked at me like she didn't understand. She wouldn't stop looking at me because she wanted to understand. I sighed and wrestled with spilling the beans about Yaris being pregnant.

I finally said, "I'm stressed right now, Mom."

"Is the coach getting on you or something? Because I can call him and we can get this thing worked out right away. I told him that my baby could play, but he isn't going to use you, abuse you, talk to you any kind of way, and make you feel worthless. I know how these football coaches can be."

"Mom, this has nothing to do with Coach. I brought this on myself."

"Okay, I'm tired of the games. What is the problem?"

I took both of her hands and said, "Yaris is pregnant."

Without flinching, she said, "And you're sure it's yours?"

"Mom!" I shouted, upset that she would even ask me that. She knew how tight Yaris and I were. Even though it would be way easier for me if the baby wasn't mine, she was out of line to suggest that it might be. And if that were the case, I would have probably been even more devastated.

She snatched her hands away from me. She began grinding her teeth. She placed her hands on her hips and started pacing back and forth. My mom was livid.

"I don't understand this, Hagen! We've talked about this. I told you to practice abstinence, and if you couldn't do that, to make absolutely sure to use protection. So how did she get pregnant?"

I was about to speak, but she cut me off. "You know what, don't even answer that. You're so excited to feel good that you don't think of the consequences. I knew I shouldn't have allowed her fast behind to be over here when I wasn't home. Leaving two teenagers in my house unsupervised was just asking for trouble. I can't believe you let this jeopardize your future. I can't believe you're doing this to me!"

"I'm not asking you to help, Mom. I don't need you to do anything. I'll figure this out."

"Oh, like that makes a whole lot of sense," she said as she threw her hands up in the air like she couldn't believe me. "You don't even have a job, Hagen. How you gonna help this girl raise a baby? And what if it's twins for goodness' sake, or triplets even?"

"Mom, what are you talking about?"

"Twins and triplets run in our family."

"But I'm not the one pregnant."

"Well, genes do crazy things! You know my cousin Hector's boy had triplets and then twins right after that."

"Okay, Mom. Okay," I said. "Sorry I let you down."

"I just hate that you won't listen to me. I was in your room the other day—"

"Mom, what were you doing in my room?"

"I was cleaning up in there, and I was shocked when I saw some porn magazines. You're just like your father. You think sex rules the world. You better learn to control that urge. How could you, Hagen? Don't you see how hard it is for me, being a single mom, trying to do this on my own? And here you go and get a girl in the same situation. Are you going to marry her? I'm not going to let Yaris raise a baby by herself, but you're not ready to marry her either. Do her parents know yet?" I nodded and looked away, not enjoying the memory of their reaction. "They didn't take it too well either, huh? Her dad must be furious with you."

"Who cares what her dad thinks, Mom?" I said, honestly mad with myself that I told her the truth, but knowing I couldn't keep it from her either.

"Oh, Hagen, you just don't know how shaky this ground you got us on is. Go … just go. I'm so disappointed in you."

I was disappointed in myself too. I really would've loved for my mom to be supportive, but it wasn't like I could blame her for not responding the way I wanted. She'd responded as well as could be expected. I'd gotten myself into a pickle. I had to talk to Yaris so we could figure this out.

I called Yaris's phone multiple times, but it kept going straight to voice mail. I just wanted to have her in my arms and make sure she was okay. As bad as my mom had let me have it, I was sure it was double trouble for Yaris. I wanted to ease some of that tension. When I couldn't get a hold of her, I decided to call one of her girls. They were like peas in a pod, and they had just won the 5A Cheerleading Championship, so surely there would be some sort of celebration. I called up Ariel.

"Hey, have you talked to Yaris?" I immediately asked when she picked up.

"You could say 'Hey, how are you doing?' " Ariel said, snapping back to me.

I wanted to tell her, "Do you think I'm in the mood to be all cordial?" But I was calling her, so I couldn't get testy.

"Hey, I'm sorry. I should've asked. How are you doing?"

"That's better. I'm fine, but I know you're not calling about me. Yaris ... you need to see her."

"Ariel, I'm asking you straight up. Can you help?"

"Well, what do you want me to do? I heard that her dad said you can't see her. You want me to put you in my purse and smuggle you into the house or something? I don't even know if he'll let us girls see her."

"Y'all are going over there?"

"We got a party tonight."

"It'd be so cool if you could work it so that instead of taking her to the party, you take her to meet me. Then I'll meet back up with you guys to get her back home. I just want to make sure she's all right because she was pretty frazzled by everything that happened this morning. I was happy she made it through the competition."

"Hagen, I'm really pissed with you. I just can't believe you didn't use protection or anything. How could you go and get my girl pregnant?"

I couldn't believe Ariel was getting all in my business. But I'd been asking myself the same question over and over again since I heard the news earlier in the day. Why hadn't I been responsible and made sure we used protection?

"Can you just bring her somewhere to meet me?" I said, not wanting to answer Ariel's question because she needed to butt out.

I knew Yaris was her girl and all, but she was my girlfriend. This was our problem. Though I needed Ariel's help, I didn't need to answer to her.

"I'll just text you if I can get it worked out."

"All right."

"Hagen!" my mom called out.

I went over to her bedroom door and saw she looked to be in distress.

"Mom, what's wrong?"

"I don't know. It's my back."

"Do you need to go to the hospital or something?"

"No, I just need to rest. Get me some aspirin and water. I'm going to lie down."

"I thought you had to go to work."

"I'm going to call in and tell them that I can't go."

I didn't want to say so, but this was a good development for me because this way if Ariel could get things worked out, I could take my mom's car to go meet up with them. When I came back into her room with the water and aspirin, she looked at me and rolled her eyes. She took the water and pills from me, but she clearly wasn't happy with me at all.

"I don't know if you got me all worked up and that's why I'm physically stressed, or what. A baby? Hagen, really?"

I wanted to say, "Mom, we've already been down this road" but I held my tongue, because we would probably keep going down this long road for nine more months. I'd definitely bit off more than I could chew. I didn't know what my mom wanted me to say. I felt bad that I let her down. I let Yaris down, and, honestly, I let myself down, being so into what I was feeling and not being responsible. I understood why her father didn't want her to see me. I'd given him my word that I wouldn't cross the line, but dang, his daughter was gorgeous. One thing led to another, and it just couldn't be stopped.

About an hour and a half later, I got a text from Ariel saying, "Meet us at the bowling alley in thirty minutes." I was so thrilled that I was going to see my girl that I didn't think to text back right away.

I was on my way when I got another text that said, "Are you coming?"

Even though I was driving, when I got to a light I texted back, "Yes." But of course, with the luck I was having lately, I was beside a cop. When he saw me texting, he put on his flashing lights.

"Are you serious?" I said to myself as I hit the steering wheel in frustration. I pulled over. I knew what time I was supposed to be there to meet the girls, but this was going to make me late. I hoped they'd just stay there and wait.

The cop walked up to the car and said, "Son, do you know why I pulled you over?"

"Yes, sir," I said.

"You know texting while driving is illegal?"

"Yes, sir," I said.

"Let me see your license and registration."

I handed them over and said, "I'm sorry, sir. It was an emergency."

"Well, I don't think it was an emergency, and it is illegal, so next time if it's that important, pull over, turn off your engine, and then handle business. I've seen so many young people lose their lives or hurt someone else because of their poor decisions."

When he let me go, I realized I should have been at the bowling alley ten minutes ago. I knew Ariel was crazy and would get mad, so before I took off, I texted her, "Got a ticket. I'm on my way."

She texted back, "Yaris is already there. We took off. We couldn't wait. We'll be back in two hours to get her. Have fun, and take care of our girl."

When I got to the bowling alley, I saw a group of motorcycles. My heart dropped as if I were on a roller coaster that was teetering on the top of an incline and about to plunge downward. I didn't even have to guess at who it was. It was the Bones, and I was by myself. I didn't have my boys there for back up, and I had no time to be timid because Yaris was standing out there. My girl was gorgeous, and they would be trying to get with her for sure. If she turned them away, it'd be crazy.

Panicked, I parked sloppily and dashed up to the front of the bowling alley. When I didn't see her there, I walked to the side. My heart stopped beating when I saw Loco with his hand around her neck and the other hand around her waist, pulling her against him. She was fighting him, looking terrified.

That was my girl, and she was carrying my baby. Without even thinking about what was going to happen to me, I tried to get him to take his hands off my girl, but it got crazy. His boys pulled a knife out on me and cut me in the arm. Yaris was crying. I was upset, but when he let us go, I knew this wasn't the end of it. Not because that was what he wanted, but because that was the way I needed it to be.

It wasn't about him disrespecting me; I wasn't trippin' over all that. But he messed with my girl. What kind of a man would I be if I didn't find his tail when he wasn't expecting it and take care of business? He had to know I wasn't a punk, or this would happen again. He'd told me if I didn't go to the police and get them to take my name off the list of witnesses set to testify against him, he would come after me, and worse, Yaris. That was what scared me. Yeah, I wanted revenge, but keeping Yaris safe took precedence. I would have to do what Loco demanded. Heck, they had a ton of evidence. Even if I didn't testify, his butt was going to jail for a long time.

"You can't take me home. Can we just talk? Let's just hold each other. Let's just …"

Yaris was really upset by all this. She wanted me to stay over, but there was no way I could. Her dad would not have gone for that. And the Bones knew where I lived, so I didn't want to leave my mom alone. I dropped her off, went home, bandaged my arm as best I could, and called my boys. They were over within the hour. Emerson and I were ready to take care of this. All he needed me to do was say the word because he was still upset about what they'd done to his father's church. But Ford and Stone wouldn't let us go anywhere. They even got Ryder on their side.

"You can't be trying to go and start a war," Stone counseled me. "Let's just lie low, think this all over, keep it together—"

"Keep it together? You should've seen what he did to me. To Yaris."

"But how is it going to help us if you're dead?" Ford said. "What is your mom going to do? How is Yaris going to feel? Quit trippin', relax, and stay solid."

CHAPTER THREE
Not Cool

When my boys finally left, I was feeling worthless. I'd done terrible in the game. I'd gotten my girl pregnant. Guys were threatening my life, and I wasn't doing anything to retaliate. My life was way too heavy. I felt like an ant trying to carry a brick on its back.

I needed my load lightened. I thought about Yaris. Since I left her with a little attitude, she might have thought I was mad at her, but really, I was just frustrated about Loco and his crew. Truth be told, she was the one who could put a smile on my frowning face and fire back into my cold heart.

All I could think about was being with her. If she was in front of me, baby or not, we'd be going to town, making out like crazy. It was so hard to not be able to see her.

All I wanted to do was try to go to sleep and not think about a thing, but I heard my mom crying. Had I upset her that badly? Had I made her world seem over? Or was her back bothering her worse than earlier in the day? I felt horrible realizing that when I'd come home, I was so into my drama that I never even checked on her to see if she was okay. She was just so quiet that I assumed she was asleep, and maybe that was my error. Had I looked in on her when I first got back, she might not be in as much pain now.

I opened up the door and walked over to her bed. She didn't even stop crying to look up and acknowledge my presence. She was that consumed by whatever was bothering her. I rubbed her back and sort of pulled her to my chest.

"Mom, it's okay. We're going to get through this. It's going to be fine. Is it me? The baby? I'm so sorry. I know this is stressful. We're going to figure it out somehow. Maybe I shouldn't have told you."

"No, no, that isn't it!" she wailed, sounding like she was in pain.

It was hard for me to see her like that, so I said, "Okay, where are you hurting? Has the pain gotten worse? Do I need to call an ambulance? Talk to me, Mom, please!"

"I don't need an ambulance."

"Okay, do you want me to rub your back some more? What can I do? Do you need more medicine?"

Before I left to meet Yaris, I didn't even think to bring more aspirin and fresh water to her nightstand in case she needed it while I was away. So it had been awhile since she'd taken any pain medicine. Maybe that was what the problem was.

Then she grabbed my arm and said, "No, no, that's not it. Here!"

She handed me what appeared to be some kind of court document.

"What is it, Mom?"

"Read it, son. It's your dad. He's suing me for alimony, as if I have anything to give him. He's going to sue me? He should be paying me to help raise you." She was ranting in a daze. "I just can't take this! I knew having a kid was wrong, but I wanted to please him. I wanted to make him happy and—"

"Wait, Mom, what are you saying?" I asked, catching her way off guard.

She finally realized she wasn't alone. She wasn't venting to herself or the air. I was in the room. I was able to hear her. Was she telling me she didn't want me? I knew she was upset, and I didn't want to make it worse, but how was I supposed to take this news? How was I supposed to be okay with what she told me? How could I deal with knowing I was a mistake, and how could I live with knowing I was making her life miserable?

"I'm sorry, Mom," I said, throwing my hands in the air.

I felt numb, like her news had shot me with novocaine in the gums as if I was about to get a filling or something. She had always been a tad reserved; she was never an overwhelmingly affectionate, loving mother, the kind who wants to hug you all the time and just be the world's greatest mom. I chalked that up to her personality, but now the truth was coming out. What do you do with a kid that you really didn't want and now feel is ruining your life?

Very saddened and truly stunned, I repeated, "I'm sorry."

I backed up and started to leave her room, but she jumped out of bed and rushed over to me. Hugging me, she said, "I'm sorry, son! I'm so sorry. I didn't mean what I said. I don't know what I was thinking. You know I love you!"

But she'd already said it, and those words couldn't be taken back. I gently pushed her away from me and went back to my room. I had to deal with what I had previously heard, and that was hard.

The next morning when I awoke, I knew I was going to have to do something to change my state of mind. I wasn't going to get depressed, though technically I really already was. I was tired of rehashing this state of my life. If I wanted it to be different, I was going to have to make it that way. I could hear my mother moving around in the kitchen. Honestly, I was salty with her. I hoped she wasn't cooking anything for me because I wasn't in the mood to eat.

I wanted to go work out, and I didn't want to ask my mom to borrow her car. I knew early every Sunday morning Ryder went to lift at the local gym, so I called his phone, hoping to catch him before he started pumping iron. Hearing his voice made me crack a smile.

"What's up, man? You're the last person I thought I'd hear from," he said, sounding all bright-eyed and bushy-tailed. That dude loved mornings.

I asked, "Hey, are you headed to the gym?"

"You know I am. Our season is over 'cause we lost the game, but I still gotta—"

"You don't have to explain all that to me," I said.

"Oh, quit being so sensitive. Nobody said anything about you or your playing. I want to play basketball, so I got to stay in shape. That's all."

Getting to the point of my call, I said, "I want to go. Can you come swoop me up?"

"I'm almost by your house. You better throw on some sweats and come on out."

"No problem."

I didn't feel like talking to my mother. I didn't want to hear her apology, and if she was not going to apologize again, I didn't feel like dealing with her attitude anymore. However, I wasn't the type of son that would leave without saying anything. On top of everything, she didn't need to worry that I would run away. While she'd let it slip that initially she might not have wanted me, I knew she loved me.

I popped my head in the kitchen and said, "Mom, Ryder's here. I'm headed to the gym. See you later."

She turned to try to say something, but I high-tailed it out of there before she could finish. Ryder talked all that junk about being right at my house, but he wasn't. I went to the corner to wait for him because I didn't want her to come out and try to start a conversation.

When he came ten minutes later, I said, "Boy, you rushed me and told me you were almost here."

"Yeah, well, I had to get me some gas. But I picked this up for you," he said as he tossed a Gatorade in my direction.

Since I hadn't eaten, that was perfect. I needed to get a little something in my system so I wouldn't get dehydrated.

"You didn't get me any food?" I said to my buddy.

"I ain't your mama … So, what's up?" Ryder said after a long pause.

Frustrated, I uttered, "Nothing. I just wanted to work out."

"You never want to get up early and work out with me. I asked you all the time last season, and you didn't want to do it. So what's up? I'm not oblivious. I know this baby thing has got you stressin'. You're gonna be all right."

I pressed my lips together real tight, pondering his words. I wasn't ready to be a dad, but that wasn't what was getting me down.

"I'm all right."

"You don't have to share it with me, but whatever it is, working out will clear your head."

I nodded. We drove in silence, and I was happy to get to the gym to let off some steam, and that I did. After a great workout of lifting one hundred fifty pounds and bench-pressing two fifty, I got into the car with Ryder to go home. I guess I looked a little somber because he popped me in the head.

"Ow! What's wrong with you?" I shouted.

"I'm trying to perk you up, one way or another."

In a not too convincing voice, I said, "I'm fine."

"Yeah, whatever, man. I know you, and you're stressed out. I'm here for you, man, for real. You know you can talk to me."

"I ain't really up for talking, but thanks for letting me tag along today."

"Maybe you need to get laid," he joked.

I punched him in the arm. Not hard enough for him to go all over the road, but hard enough for him to know he needed to hush. Maybe he was right on. I wanted to ask him if he ever made himself feel good. But though we were boys, we weren't that close, and I certainly didn't want him to think I was crossing any line. So, I just leaned back.

He said, "You know, I was just joking about you getting laid and everything. I know you're probably trippin' about your girl being pregnant and all. It's not your fault. I mean, it is partly your fault ..." he said, when I looked at him like, *Are you kidding?* "But without protection, it coulda happened to any of us. Hell, even with protection, it can happen. Things can go wrong. Some girls even try to trap guys that way, but you know Yaris. That's not her style."

"No, that's not her style," I said, getting a

little offended that he would even say that in the first place.

I wanted to talk to Ryder. So much was swirling around in my head, but I really didn't know where to start. Though the words wouldn't come, I was happy to know he was there.

When we pulled up at my house, he said, "If you want to hang out later, let me know. Some of the fellas are coming over to watch the NFL game. Falcons, baby!"

Unsure, I replied, "I might call you."

"All right, cool." We slapped hands, I got out, and he took off.

I wasn't excited to see my mom's car still parked there. She had her work schedule posted on the refrigerator, and I thought she had to leave early today. I hoped she wasn't feeling bad and decided to stay home because I really couldn't take her. Knowing that I smelled worse than a pig that rolled around in the mud and then in slop, I went straight to my bathroom to take a much-needed shower.

My mom opened the bathroom door a crack and said, "Son, I'm headed off to work."

"Okay, sounds good," I said, needing her to shut the door so I could have some privacy.

When she left, I resumed my attempt at serenity. I'd already washed myself all over, but I stayed underneath the hot water an extra minute and let it relax me. When I got out of the shower and glanced out the bathroom window, I noticed that my mom's car was still in the driveway. When I moved over a little, I saw she was talking to someone. A smile came across my face as soon as I saw it was Yaris. I hoped my mom wasn't saying anything to offend her.

I didn't know how my girl had managed to come over here since her dad didn't want her to see me. He had to have seen me bring her home. I had a feeling that she probably needed me, and as messed up as I really was, I needed to figure out a way to get it together so that I could be there for her.

Before I could apologize for the night before and make sure my mom hadn't insulted her, she gave me great news. We weren't having a baby. Just watching her lips say that was sexy to me. I wanted to pull her close, have my way with her, and escape life for a few minutes, but she wasn't having it, and I couldn't figure that out.

"Come here, baby. I'm going to make you feel good," I said to Yaris, though I really wanted her to make me feel good.

I couldn't believe she was pulling away. If there was ever a time I needed her love and affection, it was definitely now. But, doggone it, she wasn't feelin' it.

"We just got out of having a baby. I'm not trying to do something to put me at risk again," she rationalized, hoping I'd see things her way.

I took both of her hands and said, "I got you, and I understand that. I am not trying to slip up anymore. I got protection," I said.

I tried to lead her back to my bedroom, but she jerked away and stood firm. Did she want me to beg her? Was I supposed to plead? I know she didn't expect me to get on my knees. I could seduce her, but she wouldn't let me. I wasn't an idiot. I understood she was scared, but it had been a while since we'd been together. Hadn't she missed me like I'd missed her?

Standing her ground, she explained, "I'm

not doing it, Hagen. What do you need me to say? How can I make you understand I'm serious about this? Please stop pushing me. Yeah, you want to feel good. I get that, but I've been feeling horrible these last few days, thinking I was carrying your child. And I talked to your mother—"

Cutting her off, I said, "My mom? What does she have to do with this?"

"She just made a lot of sense. She said the only way to be sure our scare doesn't turn into reality is to not have sex. So back off." She pushed me back.

I guess I snapped when she rejected me like that. She was my heart, but at that moment I wanted to hurt her like she was hurting me. She knew me well enough to know that I was in agony and going through stress, and she knew that being with her, touching her, feeling her, and caressing her would take my stress away, yet she was refusing.

Seeing I was upset, Yaris offered, "Can we just talk? Can we just watch some TV? Maybe we should get on our knees and pray. I know *I'm* thankful I'm not pregnant."

Softening my tone, I stroked her cheek and said, "I'm thankful you're not pregnant too, Yaris. I mean, dang, I said I got you."

In a serious voice, she said, "I don't want you to have me like that."

"Then you know what? You need to get to steppin'," I uttered.

"What do you mean?" she cried.

"I'm putting you out," I told her.

I didn't want to cuddle, I didn't want to watch TV, and I certainly didn't want to talk. I wanted sex.

Not wanting to leave, she pleaded, "Hagen, we can talk about this. You don't have to put me out. I love you, and I know you love me. Please, Hagen. I'm your girlfriend."

Totally fed up, I said, "Right, and my girlfriend is supposed to meet my needs, and if you can't do that—"

"What? You're giving me an ultimatum now?" she asked, looking hurt.

Unmoved, I nodded toward the door and hoped she got the point. I felt a little bad as I watched her slowly turn around, walk out to her car, and drive away. However, we were on two opposite sides of this issue. I needed distance.

I spotted my next door neighbor walking her dog. All she had on was a workout bra and some skin-tight jogging pants that made her body look super attractive. Cara had a crush on me. She graduated last year. She wasn't my type because she wasn't doing anything with her life, but maybe she was just what the doctor ordered.

I opened up the door and said, "You better put on a coat. You're gonna get sick."

"What are you gonna do? Warm me up?" Cara teased as she stuck her finger in her mouth.

"I can," I told her as I licked my lips, wanting to kiss hers.

"Well, let me put this dog inside, and then we'll see. I saw your little kindergarten girl-friend leaving all stormy mad. What? You tired of holding her hand?"

"When you gonna let me hold yours?" I yelled out, not even wanting to entertain comments about Yaris Fernandez.

Playing with me, Cara seductively said, "I don't think you're ready, Hagen Cruz."

"Oh, I'm ready," I quickly told her as I held my door open.

"When is your mom coming back? She warns me all the time not to sneak over here when she's gone."

"She went to work. You know those long shifts she has," I said as I watched Cara strut as she went toward her backyard.

"Yeah. Seeing how pent up your little girl makes you, we're going to need time for me to unwind you."

"Well, quit talking. Put that dog inside and come on."

I actually could not believe that I told Yaris to leave and that I was ready to get with Cara. This wasn't about feelings; this was simply about needs. It took Cara all of ten minutes to knock on my front door. Coming to the door in my robe, I let her in.

"Somebody put a robe on over his clothes. I thought we were gonna have some fun. If you're not ready for that, call me when you are," she said, about to turn around and walk right out the door.

But I opened up the robe and showed her my bare chest and boxers. Immediately she grabbed my buns, and her luscious lips devoured mine.

I could almost pretend it was Yaris in my mind, and I wondered why I kept Cara away all this time. She was aggressive, she was feisty, and she was ready to have me.

"Hey, we're not having any strings attached or anything like that," I said as I finally pulled my lips apart from hers.

Cara confirmed, "No, I don't need any commitment. You can even keep your holding-hands girl if you want."

I held her at arm's length to make sure we understood each other. "Be sure there's no expectations. As long as you been hounding me to get this, I can't imagine once you get it you're just gonna go."

"Oh, don't flatter yourself, Hagen. Show me what you got. You're doing a lot of talking, but you ain't taking off nothing."

Yaris was about a size 6. Cara was a 10, but her curves were in all the right places. Unfortunately, she kept bringing up Yaris. I was trying not to think about my girl, but it was hard when she kept talking about her.

"I bet your girlfriend can't do this. I bet your girlfriend won't get down like that."

The more she talked about Yaris, the more guilty I felt. Yeah, I sent her packing, but getting with another girl this soon after felt wrong. I wouldn't want Yaris being with another guy. But how could I stop this moment of passion when it felt so good? Right before we went too far, I backed away and ended the passion because this was not cool.

CHAPTER FOUR

Clearly Frustrated

I didn't have time to get out of the way of Cara's perfectly manicured hand. She slapped me, and none too softly either.

"Ouch!" I yelled. "What was that for?"

"You get me all aroused. You tell me it's our time. I come over here, practically reveal all, and then you decide no thank you?"

"Hey, we agreed there were no ties here. We're both allowed to change our minds."

For goodness' sake, what was she tripping about? I didn't use her. She should be grateful. However, watching her chest heave and steam practically shoot from her ears, I knew she wasn't happy.

As she gathered her top and pants she uttered, "Don't you ever look my way again. You're such a punk. I see why you were marked in the ninth grade."

She started to open the door to leave, but I ran over and shut it. "What are you talking about? I was marked in the ninth grade?"

"Haven't you ever wondered why the Bones picked you?"

"I know why. It's because of my father. He left town and didn't pay some debt, so they look to me to pay it."

"You idiot, why do you think they reached out to your dad to help them with some money?"

"I thought he reached out to them," I said, honestly wanting to figure this whole thing out.

"You really don't know, do you?"

"No, I don't."

"Have you ever even heard of someone being marked?"

I shook my head because I hadn't.

Cara explained, "Every month the gang identifies some weak kid. The person has to be real pathetic and in need of protection, and the gang leader has to sign off on it. So they study you, torture you, go after your weakness. In your case it must have been your father. That's how they reel you in. I tried to get them to leave you alone, but now I'm glad they didn't."

I just looked at her. I was confused and upset. Processing all this info had me truly uneasy.

She got offended. "What? I'm just telling you. At first I didn't see why they picked you, but now I do. You are truly a weak, pathetic prick."

"How do you get unmarked?" I asked, ignoring her insult.

"You don't, and maybe in your case that's not a bad thing. I'm actually supposed to see Loco tomorrow."

"What do you mean you're supposed to see him?"

"We do what you wouldn't."

"You mean you're Loco's girl?" I said, feeling like I'd just been punched in the gut. "How could you be with me if you're with him?"

"He doesn't own me!"

"I know, but if he thinks he does, why would you drag me into all of that? You got to go. They could be watching you right now. Those guys are crazy, Cara!"

"Right, and I can handle my own."

"I can't," I uttered, not meaning to sound so pitiful.

"Well, you better find a way to."

With that, she opened up the door and exited. I sank back down in my chair. No need to look out the window to see if anyone was casing my joint because now it was what it was. I needed to go buy a gun. I was marked. All this time I thought I owed my father's debt, and while that was a factor, that wasn't the main reason.

I crossed the line with Loco's girl because I was so desperate to get my game on. If my life spiraled out of control because of that, then I deserved what I got. While in theory it sounded like I was prepared and could handle it, bring it on, come what may, no backing down, who was I kidding? I was petrified. They knew where I lived. They knew where my girl lived. They knew where Cara lived, and they didn't play fair. Though I felt I needed a gun, I knew I couldn't buy one. Not only did I not have any funds, I also didn't know anybody that would sell one to me.

I called up Stone and asked if he was going over to Ryder's to watch the game. He told me he was planning to chill but that he'd come pick me up if I wanted to go. I said I did. When there was a knock on my door about twenty minutes later, I grabbed my jacket, keys, and cell phone and rushed to open it. I said, "Man, all you had to do was honk, and I would have come out."

As soon as I opened the door, a .44 Magnum was pointed dead in my face. Loco and three of his goons pushed me back inside my house. I didn't know if they had come to vandalize the place and beat me up, or worse, kill me. But me being inside with the four of them was not a good thing. I was so upset internally because I had no leverage. It was just me against them, and I was no match for anybody's gun, particularly not when it was being held by someone who did not mind pulling the trigger.

"Loco, man …" I threw up my hands and tried explaining, "I did not know Cara was your girl. I was just trying to have a little fun; you can understand that. If I had known that she was yours, I would have never tried to hit that. But we didn't do anything, I swear. Your guys were casing the joint, you know. Pretty soon after she came, she was gone. Lots of guys are quick, but nobody's that fast."

Loco squinted and said, "What are you talking 'bout, man? Don't nobody care about that trick."

If they weren't here about Cara, why were they here? He could tell by my expression that I did not understand. His thugs laughed.

One uttered, "He's so dumb, Loco. You better school him. He's shaking like a little leaf. You better school him before he pees in his pants."

Loco laughed in my face. "You scared?"

"What's this about, man?" I asked, wanting him to get to the point.

"Don't be rushing me," Loco said in a heated tone. "The only reason why I'ma get to it is because I got things to do. My terms, not yours, you understand?" I nodded. "Do you understand?" he asked again.

"Yes."

"My attorney called. He said the DA hasn't gotten any new evidence, so that's good. Their case is weak. Problem is, your name is still on the list of witnesses set to testify against me. I thought we settled this."

"I just saw you yesterday, man."

"How long does it take you to talk to him?"

"It's a Sunday and—"

"So you talked to him?" Loco interrupted, cutting me off. "I'll know if you're lying ..."

I hadn't talked to the DA or the detective. I hadn't even thought about talking to them. I didn't even know if I wanted to talk to the DA to recant all that I'd seen, but with my life on the line, I had to come up with something to make Loco back off.

"It's a Sunday. I couldn't get him anyway. It's not like I have his personal cell number. I'd have to call the office, and he only works Monday through Friday. I can't call the DA. I don't even know him. I got to call the detective."

Loco looked over at one of his boys, who I guess was familiar with the system. The thug, who had his long hair in a braid, gave a slight nod. I guess it gave Loco the confirmation he needed to know that I was telling the truth.

"All right, well, we'll touch base with you tomorrow, and all this needs to be cleared up and taken care of by then. We'd hate to have to come back and ..." Loco gave his guys a nod.

One of the guys pulled a bat from behind him. I jumped back. He smashed a lamp that was sitting on one of the end tables to make a point.

"I understand," I said.

"Can't hear you ..." Loco prodded as he motioned for the guy to hit something else.

"I got this, I, I got it," I said quickly to avoid any more damage.

"All right, that's better. We'll see you tomorrow."

When they left, I stood with my back against the door, banged my head against it a couple times in sheer frustration, then slid down until I was sitting on the floor. I hated being in this situation. My life was so messed up.

My mom shouted, "Hagen, you need to come on out of there, son! We need to talk."

"Mom, I got to go to school!" I yelled from the other side of the door. I needed to hurry up and get out of there because I got up late. Plus, I wasn't eager to rehash Saturday night's revelation.

"Are you dressed, son? This door is locked; you know I don't like locked doors in my house."

It *was* her house, and she could set the rules. But I didn't want to be disturbed while I was getting ready, so I had locked my door. I wasn't unlocking it until I was dressed.

"Son! Okay, fine, I get it; you're mad at me. But you can't be as mad at me as I am at myself. I love you, and I shouldn't have made you feel like you're a mistake."

"Nothing is wrong with telling the truth, Mom!" I bellowed.

"Hagen, you know I've been going through a lot. That's the truth. Back hurting, head hurting, heart hurting ... Come on, please come out?"

Finally dressed, I opened the door and said, "Mom, you don't have to try and cover it up. If Yaris had really been pregnant, that wouldn't have been something I wanted either. I get that I was a mistake."

"Let's get one thing straight right now: you weren't a mistake. You were just unexpected. And I didn't finish the rest of that story. Carrying you those nine months gave me purpose. Up till then I was playing around, living life any old kind of way. But when I had you and I looked into those big, beautiful dark eyes for the first time, my world changed. I became responsible. I'm the assistant manager at Walmart because you came into my life."

My mom's eyes started to water. I could tell she was real sorry for the distance her harsh words had put between us. Seeing how much she cared, I removed the barrier and hugged her. She gripped me real tight. Then she spotted something in the hallway window.

She pulled back and said, "That car's been sitting there all night. It's got the mark of that gang on it. Is there something going on that I need to know about, Hagen? Are you in some kind of trouble?"

I got a lump in my throat as I vividly recalled Loco's threat. I knew today was the day he wanted some action from me. I thought he was smart enough to know I couldn't go anywhere, but to put somebody in front of my place and case it like they were the cops and I was a criminal really got me hot under the collar.

"Nah, Mom, I got this. I don't know why they're out there."

"Okay. Maybe they're visiting the people across the street."

"Yeah, that's got to be what it is," I said as I kissed her forehead.

Satisfied, my mom went off to work. A part of me didn't want her to leave. She hadn't said anything yet about her lamp being gone. I'd cleaned up the mess and dropped it in a nearby dumpster. When she noticed its absence, I had no idea how I was going to explain what happened to it, and I certainly didn't have the money to replace it.

All the way around I was up a creek, and the last thing I needed was more damage to be done by the thugs trying to come in. If they'd been casing the place, they knew I was still inside. I really hated that all my boys had a car but me, but they didn't mind trading off on picking me up so that I didn't have to be a bus rider. I couldn't think of who was supposed to be picking me up, so I texted Ford.

"You picking me up this morning?"

Ford texted back, "Nah, Ryder is."

I texted Ryder, "You swooping me up this morning?"

"Nah, I think it's Emerson," he texted back.

I texted Emerson, "You getting me this morning?"

"No, I think it's Stone."

I texted Stone.

"You got to pick me up cuz ya boy's tripping."

"No problem."

But then I thought about it. The last thing I wanted was for Stone to pull up in his shiny new ride. I picked up the phone and dialed Stone quickly as I thought about the possibilities of what might happen if the Bones started tripping.

"You know the gas station you pass before you turn in my neighborhood?"

"Yeah ..."

"I can meet you there."

"You don't have to walk all the way there. I'll be there in five minutes."

"There's a lot going on. Just don't come to my house."

He finally agreed. I went out the back door and went through the woods. I got pricked a little, but a couple scratches were way better than getting roughed up.

Soon as I got in Stone's car he asked, "All right, so what's up? Who you ditching and dodging?"

"It's the Bones, man."

"What about them?"

"They won't leave me alone. I got to get this figured out."

"Well, what do they want?"

"Loco says I gotta talk to the detective and recant my story."

"And how hard are they pressing?" Stone asked.

"Hard ..." I looked over at him and said as I took my finger and drew it across my throat.

"Oh, well then, what's the issue? Let's go by the police station."

"Nah, I'm not trying to go to the precinct. I don't know what I'm going to do, but if they catch me there ..."

"All right, all right, say no more. But I heard they're out recruiting, and they got some new guys at our school," Stone said.

"Are you serious?"

"Yeah, so you need to watch your back, front, side ... everything. And think about it. They see you at the police station, they might not think you're turning Loco in. They might think you're doing what they asked you to do."

"I don't want them to see me with you. I ain't trying to mix nobody up in all this mess."

"All right, I hear you. I hear you."

When we pulled up to school, we had to pass a whole bunch of motorcycles at the entrance. I didn't have enough time to duck down because I didn't see them at first, but they sure spotted me. My cell phone rang, and I didn't recognize the number.

"Hello?" I said.

Loco said, "I didn't think you'd be coming to school. We were waiting outside your house to give you a ride to the police station, but I see you slipped by my guys and showed up here anyway. You think I'm playing about you taking care of this today?"

"Nah, Loco, I hear you. Just got a big test this morning, that's all," I told him, saying the first thing that came to my mind.

"Right after school you handle it, because we'll be watching."

"I got you," I said before hanging up the phone.

"Was that him?" Stone asked.

"I don't want you to know nothing about this."

"Well, obviously they're watching you. They see me. We can be smart, but we don't have to run scared."

"Don't park way far out. Go close to the door so the security guard can see us and stuff," I told him.

Soon as we got in the school building, I saw Mr. Fowler, our principal. I wanted to walk up to him and tell him everything so that he could help me figure this out. But a bunch of people walking past me started looking at me crazy. I didn't know who was connected and being inducted into the Bones, and I couldn't take any chances.

Soon as school was over, I was going to have to go directly to the police station, or who knew what hell would break out. To add further insult to my injury, someone brushed past me real hard. I turned and saw it was Ariel.

"Dang, you could say excuse me or something."

"Please. Chumps don't deserve my respect."

"Yaris talked to you?" I guessed.

"She's my best friend. Of course she did."

"Where is she? I want to talk to her."

"She's gone," she said, walking away and leaving me with tons of questions.

Just when I needed Yaris, she was gone. What did that mean, gone? Gone where? Feeling like I was going to pop, I hit a locker real hard. I'd lost my girl, and if I didn't get my act together, I'd lose my life. Things couldn't get any worse.

When school was out, I asked Emerson to take me to the police station. He wrongfully assumed I was turning them in. Driving to the Cobb County PD headquarters, I realized I asked the wrong friend to assist.

"Look at you over there, all quiet ... Hagen, this is great, man! No way should he have been out on bail. Now, because he's been harassing you, we can get his butt locked up."

All I managed in return was a weak smile. Emerson read right through my silence.

He jabbed me in the arm. "What the heck, man? You not having second thoughts about doing what's right, are you?"

"No," I finally said under my breath.

"Look, Hagen, I know those guys are dangerous, and I know the last thing you want is to add fuel to the fire. But if you don't stand up to them, who will? They'll keep torturing people. You got to tell them what happened this weekend to you and Yaris. Trust me, I so wanted to retaliate when you told us about that, but this is way better. Let's beat them with the law."

Things were so complicated. After the thugs left my house yesterday, I'd just stayed in and cleaned up instead of going to watch the game. I'd texted Stone and told him not to pick me up, but I hadn't said anything about Loco's visit, so Emerson had no idea of the latest.

Tired of him pushing me to do things the way he thought I should do them, I yelled out, "I'm not testifying, okay?"

The fool slammed on the brakes. We were only going thirty miles per hour, but still. He whipped around in his seat to face me. "What do you mean, you're not testifying? Don't talk foolish. If Loco and the rest of them are pressuring you, you got to say something to the police. If you don't tell them, I will."

"Nah, you're dropping me off, and then you're gonna keep it moving. Dang, Emerson, you can't regulate my life."

"What are you talking about? Every time you need help, I'm there. Why won't you say something? Why won't you tell the police what you know? Why won't you get his butt locked up in jail? I don't understand you, Hagen! You can't just sit on the sidelines of life. This is like when they came and vandalized my church; you knew it was wrong, but you threw stuff too."

"Yeah, because they were threatening my life then, which is what they're doing again now. Don't talk about what you don't know," I said as I got out of the car.

I was miles away from the police station, but I'd be damned if I was going to sit there and get crucified by somebody who didn't know what the heck he was talking about.

"Get back in, man. We'll figure this out. I'm sorry."

Still pissed, I got back in.

"I hear what you're saying, Emerson, and I know it's right, but there's a lot going on here. I'm sorry, I didn't even think about it when I asked you to drive me. I shouldn't have because they're following and watching."

"So what?" Emerson said. "I'll drop you off, and I'll stay out of it, but I'm not going to let them control what I do, what I say, who I drive around, and how I want to handle bringing them down."

"You can say that when they ain't threatening to mess up your dad's church again or do something to your girlfriend. You didn't see what I saw the other day. I was powerless to do anything to protect Yaris against them. They know where my mom works, they know where I live, they came up in my house. I guess I was shaken."

"All right, man, all right. Handle it your way. I'm just telling you, you ain't got to go through this alone. Forget Ryder and 'nem; they want to stand on the sidelines and be punks. I'm fine with that, but this is personal for me too, and if you can't turn them in, then I don't even understand you coming to the police station."

"I won't be in there long. If you want to wait for me, you can, but you are waiting at your own risk."

"I'm at the police station. What they going to do to me?"

"I don't know, but they're crazy."

"Fine," Emerson said as he pulled up to the front door and let me out.

Once inside, I asked for Detective Frank. Luckily he was in, but unluckily for me, that meant I had to decide what the heck I was going to tell him.

"Hagen Cruz, what can I do for you, young man?"

Before I could tell him my reason for being there, he started going on and on about the Grovehill Giants football team. He said he had gone to all our games, and he talked about how he loved my playing.

"Sir, I don't mean to cut you off or any-thing ..."

"I was just going to say that I know you had a couple bad breaks there in the playoff game, and it had to be frustrating. But, you know, it's a team effort all the way around, and everybody has bad games. So I hope you haven't been beat-ing yourself up, because you're just a junior, and there's still next year."

"Oh, well, um, thank you. Sir, I ... I just came to tell you that you can take me off your witness list."

"I kind of figured. With Loco being out and on the loose, I knew that there'd be some intimidation efforts going on here."

"Just please let the prosecution know that I am not going to testify."

I got up to exit his small office, but before I could get out of the door, he stepped in front of me.

"You listen here—" he began.

"There's nothing to talk about, and you can't change my mind."

He turned around to his desk, ripped a piece of paper from a notebook, and started writing. He held it up, and it read, "Are you wearing a wire?"

"No."

"All right, then we can talk freely. You need to explain something to me. You're a big part of our case, but make no mistake about it, you're not the only part of it."

"Okay, great, so you're not going to lose anything by taking me off completely. I just need you to report that to the other side today; a lot depends on it."

"So are you telling me you've been threatened? Why are you doing this, son? You know who we're dealing with here."

"Just take me off the list."

I knew he was upset with me. But finally when he saw I was serious, he stopped pushing. Sighing, he opened up the door and let me pass through it. Emerson was still outside, but he'd moved from his spot in front of the door.

Soon as I got in the car, he vented, "Doggone cop tried to tell me I couldn't park where I wanted to park. I mean, shucks, it wasn't no big deal. He was threatening to write me a ticket. I was still in the car, and I moved as soon as he asked me to. No wonder some people hate the cops. Got such attitudes doing what they wanted to do with their lives. They should have gone into some other profession if they didn't want to maintain law and order."

"Nothing wrong with being a cop," I said.

"I know there ain't. I'm just saying, he's coming at me like he got an attitude and ain't happy with his life."

Knowing we needed to keep it moving, I said, "Let's get out of here."

"You want to get a bite to eat?"

"I'm always down for something to eat. I do need to get home, though. My mom wasn't in this morning, and she's probably got dinner waiting for me."

"All right, let's just go to the drive-through. Even if you get a little burger, you still going to eat when you get home, you greedy butt," Emerson teased, lightening up.

"Well, everybody can't be as skinny as the kickers. Thank goodness we don't eat as much as Ryder and Stone, though," I joked.

"I know that's right." Emerson paused. "So I ain't want to ask you, but you know I want to know. What did you decide to do?"

"I got to protect my family right now. I'll get it all figured out, but until I do, I got to play Loco's way. I'm not expecting you to understand."

"I got it, and I'm with you. Until we figure out another way, you did what was right."

We gave each other dap. He drove us over to Krystal's, where we both got burgers. When he pulled up to my house, there was another car in the driveway besides my mom's. "Who's at your house?" Emerson asked me.

"I don't know," I said. It made me kind of nervous to see another car there, what with all the gang stuff going on. I thought I heard some commotion from inside.

Emerson sensed my unease, so instead of leaving, he parked his car and came in behind me. I was shocked to see my dad in the kitchen. He was supposed to be in New York somewhere. He and my mom were yelling at each other. Then I saw him shove my mom, and without even knowing all of the details, I rushed over to him and started punching him.

My mom was screaming. Emerson yelled, "That's enough!" and grabbed my arms to hold me back. But it wasn't enough. So much was wrong, and my dad was just the person I needed to take all of my anguish out on. He'd made a mistake showing up here. I couldn't hold back my anger at him because I was clearly frustrated.

CHAPTER FIVE

Go Off

Hagen, calm down! Please!" my mom pleaded. There was fear in her eyes.

"Really, Mom? Are you serious?" I yelled back, seething with anger. "I came in here to find him pushing you around, and you want me to calm down? Seriously?" I shook Emerson off of me.

"You better listen to your mama, boy," my dad taunted. But he had the wrong boy because I was in the right mood to deal him another blow. I lunged at him and pinned him against the counter.

I saw my mom go over to Emerson. My buddy was hesitant to get involved any further. Finally, he did.

Emerson said, "Hagen, leave him alone. You've made your point. Come on, stop!"

I finally relented, only because I knew my dad got the message. Seeing his bruised cheek and bloody nose made me ease off. I wanted to hurt him badly, but I didn't want to kill him. My dad slumped against the countertop, and Emerson went and stood in front of him to make sure he stayed there.

"He can't even finish the job," my father had the audacity to say.

I felt my hands stinging, and I looked down at them. My knuckles were bleeding. My mom rushed over to me. "Hagen, you're hurt. Let me see, baby. Oh my gosh!"

I jerked my hands away. It seemed like nothing I did pleased her. She thought I was the worst son in America for making a mistake with my girlfriend. My very existence seemed to piss her off lately, and when I came to her defense, it still wasn't enough. Yeah, she loved me and was grateful, but couldn't she support me? Couldn't she understand how I had to come to her aid right away, seeing the unruly sight I saw? How was she going to tell me to stop when he was wrong too? He was always hitting us up for money.

Seeing I was upset with her, she whispered, "What happens if he has you thrown in jail for assault?"

"He wouldn't dare make that claim; not with Emerson standing here as a witness about what he did to you."

"Look, son, you've got it all wrong," my dad said as he tried moving from the counter, but Emerson stepped in front of him, and he stayed where he was.

My dad continued, "Your mama wouldn't listen to me. I'm not intending to go through with the suit. Her and I just need a little understanding."

"I'm not giving you a dime! There's no understanding to be had between us except the understanding that you need to get out of my house and leave me and my son alone."

"So now you care for your unplanned baby?" my dad uttered.

I was a little embarrassed that my friend was there. Having my history exposed like this made me hang my head in shame.

My mom shouted, "Shut up, you fool."

Cursing, he knocked Emerson out of the way and tried to come at her again. No way was I going to stand for that. The fight was on again.

It didn't last long, though. When a siren rang out from the street, my dad ran out the back door. Talk about being a coward. His tail sure was, and there was my mom left to tell the police there was no disturbance.

I thought that they'd automatically leave when my mom explained all was good. However, when Detective Frank came in, I knew there was more to the visit. I was just in his office, and because he heard there was trouble at my address, he was here. I felt sick.

"You can't come in," I said to him, fearing that the Bones were watching my house. But he and two other cops wouldn't take no for an answer.

"What is going on? I told you guys there was no dispute," I said. But they quickly saw that the kitchen was trashed, and they looked at me like, *Who in the world do you expect to believe that?*

Detective Frank came over to me and got real close to my face. "Look, I know the gang is tough, but you don't need to do this alone. Just tell us what happened. We'll go find them and arrest them all. I'm not going to have them threatening my witness."

"What do you mean, threatening your witness?" my mom said with utter shock on her face.

I'd decided it was best to leave my mom in the dark when it came to my plight with the gang. She had no idea what her husband or son had been mixed up in. My father was just trifling, but I was too ashamed to let her in on it. I could see her going crazy if she knew, taking matters into her own hands. She might shoot them all up or something. I was glad she worked such long hours because the last thing I wanted was for her to feel like she had to fix things.

My mom came up to me and said in a scared voice, "You're in trouble with a gang? What are these thugs holding over you? Why haven't you told me? I would've gone to the leader and pleaded for them to leave you alone." She turned to the police. "You guys are going to help my son, right?"

"Yes, all we need him to do is cooperate with us," Detective Frank said.

She sighed, seeming relieved to know they were planning to do their job and protect me. Then she gestured around her. "But all this isn't the work of a gang."

"Ma'am, with all due respect, your house didn't get like this on its own. We know this is the work of the Bones," the detective said.

"I saw that car outside of my house, and I asked you whether it was that Loco's gang sign on it," my mom said, turning on me. "You said you didn't know why they were casing the house."

"So they were stalking you? They're threatening you, right? That's why you want to recant everything," Detective Frank said to me.

Not wanting to answer, I said what was most important. "You've got to leave; you can't be here."

"We're going to put officers on this house," he tried to assure me.

"Officers can't be with my mom at work. Officers can't be with me in school, where the Bones are recruiting new guys. I've already been warned," I said in an escalated tone.

"Oh my gosh, you aren't going to school right now. This is crazy," my mom said in a panic.

"We've got him, though," Emerson stepped in and said. "We've been watching them too. We're not going to let anything happen to Hagen."

"Oh my gosh! Oh my gosh, my son!" my mom cried. "Emerson, you boys need to stay out of this."

Trying to defuse the craziness, I said, "Officers, can you please leave? This was not the work of the Bones."

"It wasn't," Emerson said, backing me up.

My mom added, "It was my husband, but I don't need you going to find him. There's nothing wrong with me."

"Mom!" I yelled out, wanting them to find my dad and throw his butt in jail.

If she knew his involvement with the gang—borrowing money from them and not being able to pay it back, giving them something to hold over my head for me to serve them all my dog-gone days—then she would want him locked up. Even though my dad was pitiful and deserved none of her sympathy, I just didn't want her to go through more than what he'd already subjected her to.

I stepped up to Detective Frank and said, "Next time you come and see my mother, if you don't want to have to tell her that her son has been murdered, I suggest you leave me alone. Just tell Loco's attorney that I've been silent."

Emerson didn't want me to stand my ground that way. Detective Frank seemed frustrated, but I had to do what I had to do for me. My dad ran out the back of my house like a coward, and that was symbolic of his leadership in our household—fleeing the moment things got rough and being nonexistent. I had to make the best decision for me and my mom. I knew Loco's threats weren't idle, and I wasn't going to give him any reason to show me the mistake I'd be making if I crossed him. So, Emerson, the detective, and the cops all left. I hugged my mom after she finally settled down. Later, I picked up my cell phone and texted the number Loco had called me from earlier. "It's done," I typed. I hit Send. Why did I feel like I sold my soul to the devil?

Days later I was happy that I didn't have to get up and go to school. It was Thanksgiving break, and, boy, it couldn't have come soon enough for me. I'd been in such a funk, and since my mother was already up and out at work, I could just chill. I woke up early, like it was a normal school day. When I realized it wasn't, I tried to go back to sleep, but I couldn't. I just started thinking about Yaris. I hated that I had been so mean, rude, and selfish. Honestly, I wondered if I needed to talk to a doctor or something. Yeah, I was a teen boy and it probably was normal for my libido to be high, but I didn't think it was cool that I couldn't control it.

The last thing I wanted to do was be anything like my father. He couldn't control his temper, his drinking, his laziness, and I didn't want any of those things to rule my life. I got my butt up and took a shower. Part of me wanted to drown my sorrows in my mom's alcohol stash. She wasn't a big drinker, so I knew the bottles she kept in the kitchen cabinet were probably full.

I started to twist open the lid of one bottle, but then I just put my head down. I was not going to cry, but I also was not going to give in. No way could I go down this dark path. That made no sense 'cause I was already on a dark path. I certainly didn't want to go deeper into this. So, I just heated up one of my mother's leftover enchiladas, pulled out a book, and started studying.

A couple hours later, my doorbell started ringing like crazy. I threw on some sweats, went to the door, and was bombarded by my boys. It was actually a nice surprise to see Ford, Ryder, Emerson, and Stone at my crib.

"What are y'all doing here?" I said to them.

"We called your cell, and you ain't called nobody back," Ryder uttered as he went to the kitchen to look for something to snack on.

I said, "My mom made some enchiladas that I just heated up. Y'all can have some of those."

"Oh, yeah," Ryder responded with glee.

Ford and Stone looked at me like I had the plague. I didn't like them checking me out so hard, but I tried not to get upset. I knew they really cared.

"Man, you know you can talk to us," Ford said.

Stone added, "Hagen, I know you've got a lot going on. But we've all had crazy stuff happen. We've gotten through it because we've been there for each other. Don't shut us out."

I dropped my head. My boys cared, but these were my issues. Last thing I needed was them getting taken down by the Bones because they helped me. I wouldn't have been able to live with myself if something happened to any of them because of me. I went over to the window to see if anyone was scouting out my place. Before I could pull back the curtain, Emerson was in my face.

"You all right?" Emerson came closer and said.

"You told them everything?" I asked, a tad salty.

He shook his head. "Nah, they've just been concerned on their own."

"Y'all don't got to be worried about me. I'm fine. I am just trying to get it together. I miss Yaris. She's gone, and I don't know where to."

Emerson uttered, "She's back."

"What do you mean?" I asked, hoping against hope that this was indeed the case.

Emerson explained, "Vanessa told me that she's back. I guess she and her family went to Texas for her cousin's funeral. He was killed by a gang."

"Oh my gosh, I had no idea," I said. The knowledge made me feel even more awful about the way I'd treated Yaris the last time I'd seen her.

"Yeah, they've been going through a tough time. But get yourself together and go see her. That'll cheer her up," Ryder said as he came back with one of my mom's enchiladas in hand.

I got my boys to drop me off at my mom's job. I got her car and headed straight to Yaris's house. I needed to apologize. I needed to make things right. I needed her to forgive me. I was nervous when I pulled up, but I took a deep breath and knew I was going to keep my cool and not leave until she knew how sorry I was.

"Hey," I said in the sweetest voice I could muster when Yaris finally opened the door.

She was stunning. She was beautiful. She needed to be mine again.

"Sorry to just show up here without calling, but I had to see you. Can I come in? I need to talk to you, Yaris, please," I said, hoping I was getting through to her.

She was looking at me like she didn't want to hear anything I had to say. I knew I'd hurt her. I'd said things I desperately needed to take back. Her cold stare said I did not have a chance.

"I need to apologize, Yaris."

She seemed to soften. I wanted to pull her close to me, and her eyes said she wanted me too. However, she didn't stand still. She was nervous around me, and I felt horrible.

"We're eating. My dad is not going to like that you're here," she said, reminding me that her father was mad at me too. "I bet he is the last person you want to be around. And I've got family here from Texas. Now is not the time for us to do this."

Yaris started to shut the door. I could not let her shut me out. I quickly put my foot in the way.

"I need to say sorry to your dad as well," I told her earnestly.

"Are you for real?" she asked me, not believing I was serious. "You really wanna speak to my dad?"

"Yes, I owe him that."

"Well, not now. We are eating dinner."

I wasn't going to be pushed off that easily. I had to stay and fight for her and make this right. I understood her apprehension. However, I could not let this go.

"Check with your dad," I said as I stepped closer, "and please try to find it in your heart to give me another chance."

I took her hand. I hoped she could feel how much I cared and how much I meant my current words. She turned away. I was getting to her. I could tell she still cared for me. She let me in, but she didn't say she forgave me.

"Daddy!" she called out. I followed her into the kitchen.

"Yaris, what is it?" her father said as he hurried around the corner. Then he saw me. "Oh no, not you. Why are you here?"

Trying to stop myself from shaking, I manned up and said, "Mr. Fernandez, if you don't mind, I'd like to speak to you for a minute. I hate interrupting your dinner, but I have not been able to sleep knowing how much I messed up. I have wanted to apologize for a while. Yaris's friends told me what happened with your nephew. I'm sorry for your loss, and I'm sorry I didn't keep my word when it came to my relationship with your daughter. I hate that I broke your trust in me."

"Okay," Mr. Fernandez said as he nodded. "I appreciate you coming here and saying this to my face. I'm still very disappointed in you, but come on in. Let's get past this. Come meet my nephew and my niece."

I was stunned he was being so cool. I knew I always liked the man. He was fair, and he believed in second chances.

Yaris looked at her father in disbelief. She didn't look happy that I was coming to dinner. I didn't understand until I turned the corner and laid eyes on a girl who was stunning. I saw Mr. Fernandez's nephew, but the girl was blushing my way, and Yaris did not like the stare of interest I was receiving.

I was introduced to Yaris's two cousins. George looked to be a couple years older than me, and he had a strong demeanor. Gigi was a hottie, but she was really starting to make me uncomfortable with the way she kept looking at me like I was on her mind for dinner.

"Cool, your cousins are here," I said to her.

"Yeah, now sit down and eat something. You're looking skinny, boy," Mr. Fernandez hit me on the back and said.

I sat right between Yaris and Gigi. It was weird having her cousin constantly looking my way. Shucks, I wasn't blind. The girl was hot. If my boys were here, they'd want me to man up.

Trying to acknowledge her, I said, "Gigi, you're very pretty ... like Yaris, of course."

"You're cute too," she leaned in and said. "And sweet."

When Yaris's little sister started coughing pointedly, I looked at Yaris and was not happy to see she was mad. But I'd only said a kind word. I now knew I could not make matters worse by being real nice to her cousin.

"Mrs. Fernandez, thanks for allowing me to stay for dinner. Have you been okay?" I asked, trying to break the tension.

Her mom said, "I've been all right, thanks. You know you are welcome here as long as you are a gentleman. It's good to see you."

"So, Mr. Cruz," her father said, "I'd like for you to show my nephew around town, if you don't mind."

"For sure, sir. I'd love to hang out," I replied.

I made sure George was cool with it. When he agreed, Gigi wanted to come too. Yaris didn't seem happy about that. Thankfully all four of us went out to the bowling alley. Gigi continued flirting. Yaris got pissed. We decided to leave as soon as the game was over.

I took them all back to Yaris's house, but George wanted to hang some more. We'd bonded a bit at the bowling alley when the girls were off catfighting somewhere. Needing to talk to someone about how I was feeling, I agreed. Gigi wanted to come. None of us were having that. At first I thought Yaris was exaggerating about how her cousin was, but I was starting to believe that the girl did not have any boundaries.

Sensing my concern about Yaris, George said, "No need to stress, man. My cousin's going to be all right."

"Can I be frank with you?" I said to this new guy I barely knew, but with whom I felt real comfortable.

George nodded. "Sure."

"I pushed your cousin away at a time when she really needed me. I didn't even know she was dealing with the loss of your brother. I'm so sorry for all your family's been going through, and as a boyfriend I shouldn't have put her through that."

"I haven't been around Yaris a lot in the last couple of years, but I've known her all my life," George said. "And I've never seen her so into a guy. You're not the first guy who has taken a girl for granted, but us guys can turn things around. Particularly when we really want to fix it, so don't give up," he said, making sure I heard him and was going to comply. When I nodded he continued. "And my sister ... she's a handful. Don't get caught up in her beauty. She'll get you in trouble."

"I was just trying to be a gentleman."

"I'm just telling you. Getting too chummy with her only backfires."

"I got you. Where do you want to go?"

"Nowhere. I'll just go riding. Whatever you think I need to see ... different parts of town I need to hit, parts I need to stay away from. My uncle will kill me if I'm in the wrong place and wind up in trouble."

"Your uncle is great."

"Yeah, he is. I actually miss my talks with him. I'm glad I'm here," George said.

"I miss my talks with him too, but I think I ruined that," I said.

"He wouldn't have let you in the house if you'd ruined the relationship. You couldn't have stressed him out more than my brother and I have over the years. Now it seems like my sister is trying to go for her turn."

"It can't be that bad."

He just laughed. "Are you low on gas?"

"Oh snap," I said looking down at the meter and seeing it was past E—and not in the right direction.

As soon as I pulled into the local gas station, I wanted to pull right back out as the Bones rolled in. I went to open up the gas cap on the car, and a gang member shut it tight. I reached for the gas handle, but my hand was shoved back. I went to try to step around the one leaning against my car so I could go inside. Hopefully they'd leave. But he put his foot in front of me, and I could not move. Just as one was about to shove me, George jumped out of the car.

"What the hell is going on?" George shouted,

pulling out a gun from his waistband and cocking it. "I suggest y'all step back. I don't know what y'all think my man did, but he's just a high school kid, and I'm sure he didn't mess with nobody. If you got some beef, I'm taking it on, and you don't want to mess with us."

"Yeah, and you don't want to mess with them," I said to George. "Just get back in the car. I'm all right."

"I'm not going nowhere, and they need to back off before I really go off."

CHAPTER SIX

Surely Mad

I could almost see steam piping from George's ears. Clearly, he was upset. He was waving a gun around at strangers he had not met. I didn't know how things went down in El Paso, but here, though you stood up for your own, you needed to know the way of the land, and two men against the army that the Bones had on their side was just not a good idea.

Naturally I was furious that the gang was flexing its muscles. I appreciated George having my back. However, he didn't know what was in store for him, and now he made things worse.

"Come on, George. Put it down, man. Put it down. There are cameras all over this gas station, and you just got to town. Put it down."

"You better listen to your boy Hagen," one of the guys from the Bones, whose tattoo read Bacon, yelled out. "I don't know where you come from, but here what you're doing is not a good idea."

"Do I look scared?" George said. I had to admit, he did not.

Bacon gave a signal and said, "No, but you need to be."

Suddenly out came four guns pointed at us. I threw up my hands. Thinking of how this could play out was frightening.

"Come on, guys! Come on everybody. Let's just pretend none of this happened. I'm gonna take my boy and go," I screeched, hoping they'd all take heed and chill.

Bacon wasn't heeding anything I said. "You can talk some sense into him, but you aren't going nowhere. Loco is on his way here, and when he finds out—"

"Loco? Is he loony or what?" George started laughing and joking about the name.

Actually, George must have been the loony one to push the wrong buttons with these guys. Didn't he know I knew what was up? What he thought was a good idea was really a very bad idea. Couldn't he tell from my demeanor that he needed to freakin' chill? I was so caught up in the moment that I didn't even realize that Loco had pulled up. He was on the side, and he blew a finger whistle.

"Don't even think about going nowhere," Bacon said to me as I started to ease into my mom's ride.

Quickly, I went around to George's side. "I know I'm just meeting you and all, but you're acting like a punk. You don't know these guys."

"I don't have to know these guys to know they're uptight. And there's no need for us to buckle. I don't go down like that," George said. "No running away in me."

Needing George to know I had a long history with the Bones, I shared, "They've been messin' with me for a while. I've gotten out of their way. I don't need you making it worse. I can handle this."

"You can handle this, but you can't get gas. You can't go in and pay. You can't leave until they say you can. You're just gonna stand there and let them intimidate you? That's your way of settling this?" George confronted me and said.

There's no way I could respond to that. I just hoped that Loco had gotten my message confirming that I'd done what he asked and told the detective to withdraw my name from the witnesses list. If Loco knew, maybe he hadn't had a chance to tell his boys yet. There had to be some explanation as to why I was still being pushed around and targeted.

"It's not adding up for you, is it?" George said, somehow reading my thoughts.

Needing George to understand he was making matters worse, I said, "They are for sure not gonna go away now with you pointing guns and stuff, man."

"Chill. Nobody got shot … yet. Besides, what do you expect me to do? They won't even let us leave. What does this Loco guy have on you anyway?" George asked me.

Shrugging my shoulders, yet knowing the answer, I reluctantly responded, "I just got marked. My dad took out a loan with them and then fled the city. So they put the debt on me and held it over my head to make me do stuff for them. These dudes are bad, for real. Bodies droppin' so fast, the families can't even bury folks."

"You must not know where I come from," George said, appearing unfazed by what I'd told him about the Bones. "My brother got killed by bad dudes, and he wasn't too clean himself. I didn't move to Georgia just to have more of the same."

"Well, then you'd better listen to what I'm saying. I'm telling you this Loco guy is crazy."

"That's what I said. He is loony."

"But you can't tell them that," I hissed, irritated that George wasn't getting my point.

George put his hand on my shoulder and said, "Look, all I'm saying is when you act weak, they treat you weak."

"But I want to live, so I'm not acting stupid," I said, shoving his hand off my shoulder. I didn't want to be punked by the Bones or by George.

"Usually when there's a deal, it's honored. If you took your name off the list for testifying, and that's all he asked of you, then your dad's debt should be wiped clean. If that's not the case, then we need to find out why. Otherwise, they're just messing with you without cause, and I won't tolerate that."

We saw Loco and the rest of the Bones heading toward us. I was fervently hoping that someone inside the gas station or at one of the other cars pumping saw and would call the police or something. However, the Bones had folks everywhere and no one wanted to interfere because no one wanted to be next.

"Hey, what's the problem here?" Loco said in a jovial tone as if he just wanted us all to get along.

George gave a start and squinted more closely at Loco. I couldn't believe he was squeamish. Yep, he talked all that noise, but now that the big man was walking our way, he was losing his nerve.

"You can't back down now," I uttered.

"What are you talking about?" George asked.

I explained, "Your face is all tensed up, and you're jumpy."

Quickly he replied, "Not because I'm scared. I'm trippin' 'cause I think I know that dude."

"Loco?" I asked, wanting to be certain he meant who I thought he meant. "You think you know him?"

Still squinting at the leader of the toughest gang around, George said, "They didn't call him Loco back home."

George's response made me wonder if he had the right person. However, as Loco got close to us, he seemed like he knew George too. Seeing their looks at each other, I knew they were not strangers.

"What's up, Lil Peanut?" George said as he nodded at Loco.

Loco's guys didn't know what to make of it when Loco paused. We all wondered how he'd react to being called Lil Peanut. But he studied George some more and when he recognized him fully, the two embraced. It was crazy beyond anything I could have imagined. It was like they were from the same place and knew the same people. They just kept talking.

It all seemed cool until Loco's thug Bacon stepped forward and said, "You may know him, but he pulled a gun on us, homie, and I ain't at all cool with dat."

"Y'all just stay back," Loco said. He asked George what the trouble was. "You bringing Texas problems to Georgia?"

"Nah, but you know how it is. You mess with one of our own, we gotta stand up. I thought you moved to Mississippi," George said, going back to them knowing each other.

"I did when I first left El Paso, but they needed me to run some territory up here in Georgia. I should've stayed where I was, though, you know? How's your brother, Jimmy?"

"Johnny," George said, sort of tripping that Loco had it wrong.

Having an "ah-ha" moment, Loco said, "Yeah, Johnny."

"He's gone, man," George revealed, sounding a bit melancholy.

Seeming to genuinely care, Loco said, "Nah, man. For real?"

"Yeah, just last week."

Placing his hand on George's shoulder, Loco said, "Dang, man. I heard those streets ain't nothing to play with down there."

"Yeah, so, why you up here wreaking havoc?"

"Just trying to make a little paper …"

"Loco," Bacon called out, sounding upset.

"Didn't I tell you to wait over there? Come on, George, let's rap." The two of them walked toward the road.

When Bacon came closer, I could see he had a swollen eye. Trying to be cordial, I said, "I'm Hagen, and are you Bacon?"

"You don't need to know my name. But you're about to get to know my gun real well—"

"Hey, hey, hey," I said, needing Bacon to simmer down and not be so hot off the frying pan. "Clearly this is a misunderstanding. Loco knows my friend George. Everything is going to be fine."

"No, it doesn't work that way with me," Bacon argued, not wanting to settle down.

"Oh, it works exactly that way," Loco said as he and George walked back toward us. "I worked it out with my homie from Texas. We gonna leave Hagen alone. He made good on our arrangement. No one needs to bother him. We honor our word. I know I taught y'all better than that."

He slapped Bacon upside the head. George motioned for me to pump some gas. I quickly did, and once I finished, we were outta there. I wanted to ask him how he'd worked it out and what he'd said, but since he didn't offer up any details, I just told him thank you. Then I dropped him off at Yaris's home. Sometimes a man needs to know when to count his blessings and leave well enough alone.

Over the next couple of days, George and I were tighter than two shoe laces tied up on tennis shoes. I felt indebted to him. Turns out he needed my help too.

"Anything, man," I said to him. "You got me out of a real jam. What do you need?"

It took him a couple of minutes to tell me. "I just didn't want you to think I needed something from you," George explained. "But I do need something from you. It's just that I would've helped you out regardless."

"I got you, man," I admitted, not tripping about giving.

"I want to help my uncle. I got to get his restaurant back on top, and I got a few ideas that I think you can help me execute because you know people," George shared.

"Okay, great, because I don't know anything about restaurants. But I do know some people around here. What are you trying to do?"

"I want to get your friend whose dad is a singer to come to the restaurant."

"Oh, cool. Sure. I don't know if he'll do it for free or charge, but let's call him up."

So I dialed Stone and told him all of what was going on. Thankfully his dad happened to be around, and he got on the phone with George. I didn't hear all of the conversation, but I could hear some of it, and George seemed pleased.

"Yes, sir … For sure, I understand," George said. "Okay, if you could plan on it, that would be great…. Oh, that's a good idea! Okay, thanks."

"What did he say?" I asked George when he hung up.

"He told me that he thinks it'll be good. However, he feels if we had a cause—a charity event—it would be a great help for the business and for the community. He thinks a cause would really get the community out to show its support, and it may get someone to help financially with my uncle's restaurant."

"What are you going to come up with?" I asked, getting that George was creative.

"I don't know. We can come up with something."

He put me in it. We could come up with something. I was down with that. I scratched my head and suggested cancer or domestic violence. We just happened to be passing a funeral procession of a kid who died a couple weeks back. But because the family couldn't afford his funeral costs, it was delayed. I explained all that to George. An untimely death can be a financial burden. Then it hit us, and we realized where the money had to go: poor families who have to bury relatives who were victims of gang violence.

"Trust me, most people should have life insurance, but they don't," George said. "I know firsthand it's hard losing loved ones, but it's even worse if you don't have the money to put them in the ground. It's even worse if they leave you with a bunch of bills; it's just crazy. I've seen people in El Paso who lost their house because a loved one died and there was no income coming in. If we can set aside a fund to help families of victims of gang violence, then not only can we create awareness of the tragedy, but we can do some good in the midst of a bunch of sorrow."

"I agree. What else did he say?" I asked, remembering there was more to the conversation.

"He suggested we make it fun and festive."

"I know that Ariel's dad owns a winery." George looked at me nonplussed. I explained, "Ariel's this girl at school who's friends with Yaris."

"Oh, nice! Let's call her up to see if her dad wants to do a tasting or if he has any new wines he wants to sell at a discounted price or something," George suggested.

So we called Ariel, and she was all in, even though at first she wasn't real happy to talk to me. But when she saw I was trying to do something good for her girlfriend's family, she was all for it, which I appreciated.

George explained to Ariel, "I just need to find a way to get the word out about it because I don't want it to be just a good night; I want it to be ongoing. I want people to know that Mr. Fernandez is struggling, and he is also trying to do good for the community. Then they'll come."

"Then we need to call my other girlfriend Skylar," I heard Ariel say through the phone.

George asked, "This girl Skylar, her dad is a local anchorman? ...Yeah, that's perfect."

The next day the plan was in motion, and I was excited to go see him carry it out. But I knew things with Yaris were on thin ice. I needed to fix that. Yaris's sister was having a coming out party. I hadn't officially gotten an invitation, but I hadn't been told to stay away. So I went. I was a little late because I had to take my mom to work first. When I got there, the program had already started. Yaris's cousin Gigi met me at the door.

"You can't come in now," she said as she put her hand in the middle of my chest.

I felt a little uncomfortable. I could tell her eyes wanted something from me; something I did not want to give. I moved out of her way, but she followed too close behind.

"You got to back up," I told her, hearing Yaris in the back of my mind saying, "Don't lead my cousin on." While I was flattered before that the girl liked me, she was getting a little too close.

When she leaned in to kiss me, I was stunned. Before I could push her away, Yaris was there, livid, frantic, and completely upset. Her cousin was smiling.

I was so disappointed and disgusted. Gigi appeared not to care. She just smirked and tried to hold on to me. When I finally got her hands off of my body, I tried to follow Yaris. I caught up with her just as she was trying to open the door, and I begged her to hear me out.

Her dad appeared at the door, got in between us, and said, "You need to leave."

"No, sir. I can explain."

Mr. Fernandez pointed to the parking lot and demanded, "You need to get out of here right now."

George came over and asked, "What's wrong?"

"He's leaving," Yaris's dad said.

Feeling horrible, but not wanting to make their special night worse, I reluctantly left.

It was Wednesday morning, the day before Thanksgiving, and the day after the quinceañera where I got dismissed like some thief who stole. I had no idea who was at the door, but I wanted the banging to stop. When it didn't, I pulled myself out of bed, realizing that my mom had already gone to work. I pulled back the curtain and saw Mr. Fernandez standing at the door with his arms folded. A lump developed in my throat.

I figured if I didn't answer, he'd go away, but I couldn't close the curtain fast enough before he saw me looking.

"Open up!" he huffed impatiently. I did. "Can I come in?" he asked, looking at me like he wanted to kill me.

I mean, he'd already put me out of his daughter's party. His other daughter had told me she didn't want to see me anymore. I had already been humiliated for something I didn't do. I didn't want to be clobbered any further. But I still felt bad about breaking my promise to him, and I knew I couldn't be disrespectful. He'd invested too much in me for me to be rude like that, so, though I didn't want to, I opened the door and gestured for him to come in.

"I didn't see your mom's car. Is she at work?"

"Yes, sir," I said, not really up for small talk.

"All right, well, I won't be too long. Usually I like to call before I just pop by, but I really need to talk to you."

"Sir, if I could just explain—"

"No, no, I came by to see you. I'm the one who needs to do the talking."

I thought to myself, "Drilling me is really what you want to do," and I didn't feel like hearing it. I mean, he was just assuming that I was the bad guy. I knew Yaris was his precious baby, and I knew we had caused quite a scene at his younger daughter's big soiree, but didn't he give me any credit? Though I let him down, didn't he still believe I was good? I hated that he didn't seem to know I wouldn't intentionally hurt Yaris like that. But who was I kidding? I deserved for him to go off on me. I *had* hurt Yaris by shutting her out when she didn't want to hook up.

I told her if she wasn't giving it up, that I didn't want any part of a relationship with her. Had she told her father that? Figuring I might as well let him go off on me so we could get it over with, I said, "I'm sorry, sir. Go ahead."

"May I sit?"

"Yeah, sure."

But I did not want him to. I mean, how long was the tongue-lashing going to be? It was bad enough that I had to put up with it. He didn't need to get comfortable to yell at me. I was trying to keep a poker face with no emotion because I'd already been broken enough for the last two days, and I didn't need him clobbering me more. I mustered up enough strength on the inside to be ready for whatever he had in store. He sat but didn't speak at first. He seemed to be chewing over something in his mind. So I prompted him.

"Yes, sir?"

"I just came to apologize."

I couldn't believe what I was hearing. I was trying to show no emotion, so I didn't respond. I just stood still, leaving him to go on and explain what he was apologizing for.

"I was wrong to jump to conclusions without hearing everything that went on last night. My nephew laid into me pretty hard, telling me that you are a young man of good character and that I should have at least listened to your side of the story. But I just assumed you were in the wrong. And my niece, Gigi, admitted that she was coming on to you, and Lord knows, she's been through so much lately. I'm not making any excuses for her, and she and Yaris are going to have their own issues trying to work things out, but I owe you a face-to-face apology.

"You and I always had a good relationship until recently. You manned up, came to me, and I accepted your apology for doing things with my daughter that I wish you guys had waited to do. I told you I accepted your apology, but maybe I was still harboring some of those feelings. I just wanted you to be a bad guy, and when I saw Yaris crying and upset, I overreacted."

Then he looked away. He was still sitting on my couch, but he couldn't face me. I knew that it must have taken a lot for him to come all the way to my house and confess that he was wrong, and it just meant so much to me because I admired him so. Now he was before me, letting me know that he wasn't perfect.

He looked back over to me and said, "Do you accept my apology, son? Do you forgive me? I pushed you out of the restaurant in a pretty cruel way. What you had to endure wasn't fair for anyone to go through, and I can't undo it, but I do want to try to fix it."

"I'm just glad you know I wasn't trying to get with Yaris's cousin. I'm just not like that, sir. Of course, any guy would be flattered that a cute girl thinks he's all that. But for you to tell me you're sorry ... it just ... I don't know." I was getting a little emotional. "It's hard to express how much you being here and saying those words means to me."

I went over to the window because I didn't want him to see me tearing up, but I could hear him getting to his feet. He touched my shoulder and said, "Son, talk to me. Tell me what's going on with you."

I just wanted to release the bitterness I was feeling. I just needed him in my life at that moment because all the anger needed to be released, so I said, "I don't know, sir. I just feel like my life is falling apart. I hate that my mom has to work herself to the bone. I'm unable to help financially, and a part of me feels like I should just drop out of high school and forget going to college so I can man up and help. My dad is a deadbeat who puts us in more debt and wants to take my mom to court so she can pay him. I'm just ... I'm angry, and I don't know how to fix my problems, so I think about getting releases in ways that aren't healthy. You're my girlfriend's father, so I don't want to talk about all that."

"No, I understand. You need an outlet," he said, trippin' me out but confirming I was talking to the right man. "There's always going to be something in life, Hagen. My business isn't going well. I just lost my nephew. My mom wants me to move my family back to Texas …"

I freaked out at hearing that because I didn't want Yaris to leave. I jumped up and put both my hands on my head. He could tell I could not take it.

"Calm down," he said. "No need to worry. We're not going anywhere. My point to all this is that there's always going to be something, and you've got to figure out a healthy way to deal with life, or you're always going to be surely mad."

CHAPTER SEVEN
All Works

Thanks for opening up," Mr. Fernandez said. "You can talk to me anytime. You don't need to keep stuff bottled up inside."

"I'm just glad we could work things out because I have always enjoyed talking to you. And while I'm glad I'm not going to be a father right now, when I thought I was, trust me, I was praying that I'd be one like you," I told him truthfully, really wanting him to know how much I respected him.

"That means a lot," he said. "Sometimes we've got to be a father to ourselves. I was in the same boat as you when I was your age. My dad died when I was young, and I was bitter at first, wondering why life was so bad, why my mom had to work so hard to provide for me and my brother. It seemed like there were always obstacles coming our way. Nothing was working. We got kicked out of one place and had to go to another and another. We ended up living in Juarez, Mexico, in the midst of trouble because that was all she could afford. I vowed that if I ever got out of there, I would never look back.

"My brother, on the other hand, got lured in, so it is a personal choice of how you respond to things that happen to you in this world. But any young man who's going to take an interest in my daughter, for a day or for a lifetime, needs to be a man who's not on the side of what's fun, fast, and flashy, but on the side of what's good, lasting, and right. You're more of a man than a boy now, Hagen Cruz. Act like it."

"I got you, sir. Thank you for the real talk," I said as I gave him dap and a guy hug.

After Mr. Fernandez left, I went into the bathroom to take a shower. I'd told George I would help him get ready for the big shindig at the restaurant later this evening. He was coming by to pick me up in a little while. But before I could get into the shower, the pounding on my door started up again. Thinking that Mr. Fernandez must have left something, I threw a bathrobe on and quickly went to answer it. I was shocked to see Loco, Bacon, and two other thugs. Without waiting for an invitation, they bulldozed their way in. Thinking of what Mr. Fernandez just told me, I knew I needed to man up.

"What the heck? Get out of my house," I said.

"Boy, please," Bacon said, looking at me like I was talking stupid.

"Why are you here looking all serious and stuff?" I said, crossing my arms over my chest and demanding an explanation. "I thought we had a truce, Loco. What's up? Why are you at my crib?"

"I don't have time to answer questions. Get on some clothes and let's go," Loco demanded as Bacon harshly grabbed my arm and pushed me toward the hallway.

"I'm not going nowhere," I tugged away and told them boldly.

Bacon started using profanity and getting real hyped. His black eye looked even worse in the daytime. He opened up his jacket and revealed a gun.

Loco came close and his demeanor changed from nice to nasty. "When I tell you to move, I'm not playing. We have business today. The truce is off. Somebody is planning to attack a shipment of mine, and I need to have extra bodies there to defend my stuff."

"But why me? I don't want to shoot a gun," I declared. I never wanted to end a life and have that on my conscience.

"Dude, it's either shoot or be shot. The freakin' choice is yours," Loco said as he stepped back and motioned for Bacon to take over.

Bacon stuck his gun in my back. I turned around and flexed to show I had a problem with it. Bacon pushed me hard in the stomach with the gun. I had no choice.

Walking toward my room, I asked, "Can I get dressed in privacy?"

Bacon kicked my door open and said, "You can get dressed, but ain't no privacy allowed when the Bones are around. I need to make sure you don't take your cell phone or nothing."

I wanted to call George. Heck, I wanted to call Detective Frank, but the gang was watching my every move. All I was allowed to take out of the house were the clothes on my back. Once we were in the car, I was able to piece together what was going on by listening to Loco and Bacon's conversation. Loco was expecting a shipment of guns, but there was another gang coming from South Carolina that was planning to seize it.

They took me to a warehouse where I was told to go into a room. Inside were a bunch of young high school cats. I recognized five of the guys from Grovehill. The others were from neighboring schools. It was a mess; they were going to put guns in the hands of inexperienced teenagers and force us to defend them against thugs who definitely knew what they were doing with firearms.

Bacon came in and said, "Everyone take a piece."

There were sixteen windows in the place. He ordered us each to cover one. They didn't know which side the gang from South Carolina was coming to or if it would be there at all, but we were told to shoot if we saw any mischievous behavior. We sat there on stakeout for an hour, and things began to unravel in the warehouse. All of our faces were white with fear, and several of the guys looked like they wanted to cry. We really needed to call the police, but there was no way to communicate with the outside world. None of us had been allowed to take our cell phones. There was no way to flee because if we stepped outside of the warehouse, we'd be shot. Though we were armed ourselves, we couldn't shoot our way out because the Bones were no doubt much better marksmen than we were. The only thing I could do was keep the guys inside calm.

"I'm not trying to kill nobody," one guy yelled out.

"Well, shoot at the ground," I said. "We're not murderers. We're not like these guys. Let's just scare the other gang, or don't shoot at all if you're unsure. We're going to get through this."

A big eighteen-wheeler showed up. With the other Bones' members surrounding him for backup, Loco walked over to the big rig. From my position I could see money exchanged and a large crate unloaded.

"Somebody's riding up from the east!" one dude called out. "Looks like another car is behind him, and it is flying."

I ran over to his window to look, and I saw

the two cars. I knew if we didn't warn Loco and things went south, he'd come after us all. I fired a shot off in the air. But before the truck could back out and Loco and his crew could react, sirens went off, and the cops swarmed in.

It was a setup. They got the South Carolina gang for carrying drugs, the truck driver for carrying illegal firearms, and Loco and his crew for being involved in the buy. When I saw Detective Frank burst into the warehouse, I rushed over to him to explain that all of us inside were innocent, but he calmed me down and assured me that he knew that to be the case.

"How?" I asked.

Detective Frank explained, "Your mom let me bug your house, and we've been following Loco since we let him go."

"So that's why he's been out," one of the high school guys said.

"Yeah, and what with recruiting you under-aged guys to do his dirty work and now catching him red-handed in the act of multiple felonies, you all won't have to worry about him running a gang in this area or anywhere else for a long time. The Bones are over."

I was relieved. Keeping my cool and helping others do the same paid off. It all worked out.

When the police dropped me off at my house, I was ecstatic. Finally, I was through with Loco and the Bones. I wouldn't have to testify; they had hung themselves. They wouldn't be able to torture anyone else, and, boy, was I relieved. As soon as I walked into the house, I wanted to drop down on my knees and say a prayer of thanks for getting out of all these close calls with the baby, with the law, and with my girl. Well, things really weren't great with me and Yaris, though her dad understood. Somehow I was going to have to make her understand too.

Before I could pray, my phone started ringing. I grabbed it and noticed I had tons of missed calls.

"Dang, there you are. Where have you been?" George stated with panic into the receiver.

"It's been a long day. You don't even know."

"You going to be able to get your mom's car to come over here? I came by to pick you up before, but nobody was home, and I can't get away now.

We have a lot to do for tonight. I need you to help me pull this off."

With all that I'd been through, I'd forgotten that I was supposed to help him draw a crowd to the restaurant. My mom would be off work soon. So I told him if she did get home as scheduled, I'd be able to keep my word and help him.

"Well, you need to tell me something. You been M.I.A. all morning. Where I come from, partners don't leave each other high and dry," he said. I could tell from his voice he was clearly upset with me.

As bad as I wanted to put all the craziness that happened behind me, George did deserve an explanation. So I said, "I had a run-in with Loco."

"I don't understand." When I told him the whole story, he gave me grace. "Dang, man. That's a trip. But they did catch him?"

"Yup."

"No way."

"I swear they caught him and some of his crew too."

"That's what's up," George uttered, sounding genuinely relieved that I was okay and that Loco and the Bones would be off the streets.

"Yeah. I got a clean slate, and I am ready to do something good with it. As soon as my mom gets in, I'll head your way."

My mom kept the place pretty clean, but I knew she'd been tired and stressed out with all she'd been going through with my dad and the lawsuit. So I started cleaning up around the house. When she came in, she was pleasantly surprised to see me hard at work mopping the floor.

"Okay, what do you want?" she asked as she raised her eyebrows.

"I want you to not have to work so hard. I want you to be taken care of. I want you to know I care. Sit down," I said, taking her purse and sitting her down at the kitchen table.

"What are you going to do? Pour me a glass of water and give me a pedicure?"

"If that's what you want, sure. Although I'm not sure how good the pedicure will turn out."

"No, I'm just kidding with you, but I am curious as to this turnaround. Usually you're in your bed moping or something. I'm not trying to judge; I've just been really worried about you, son."

"I know, Mom. I've been worried about me too. I guess I just realized that if I want my life to get any better, I've got to stand up and take charge and go after what I want. I have to learn how to be a man regardless of whether I have a role model or not."

"Oh, I like the sound of that." She hugged me. "It's Thanksgiving break. I know you don't plan on staying cooped up with me all night."

Seeing an opportunity, I seized it. "Can I use the car?"

"Oh, that's a problem. I'm pulling a double shift tonight to try to make some extra money for Christmas. I just came home for a little break."

"Mom, I don't need anything," I told her.

"Well, I hope you don't *need* anything, but a mom can give her son something he wants, right?"

"Well, can I use it for a couple hours before you go back?"

"Yeah, I just need you to be responsible and bring it back so I can get to work."

I called George to tell him I was on my way and then took off. Twenty minutes later I pulled up at the restaurant. I helped him run tons of errands for the night's event. We dropped things off at the restaurant and put them in the back when his uncle wasn't looking.

"How are you going to pull all this off if he's here?" I asked George.

"He's taking a break soon and won't be back until later tonight."

"Oh, two shifts a day?" I said, laughing.

"Yeah."

For sure our culture knew how to work. I needed to adopt some of that good work ethic. Mr. Fernandez was a worker, but he needed a break.

"So you're not going to be able to come back?" George asked.

"Yeah. And I don't even know if your cousin wants me to come back."

"You're talking stupid. Of course she does."

"Then I'll be back."

Before I left him at the restaurant, I said, "And thanks for telling your uncle the truth about what really happened with me and your sister."

"Man, the truth will always set you free, right?"

I was really learning a lot. That you have to treat people the way you want to be treated. That you have to protect your true friends and go out of your way to make sure they're okay. That you have to let people you care about know how much they mean to you. That was what I was planning to do from now on: drop the pity parties and man up.

When I walked into the restaurant later that evening, I spotted Yaris from across the room. She looked so gorgeous. She looked up, and our eyes met. When she smiled my way, I hoped we'd be okay.

I knew that I'd hurt Yaris by cutting her out of my life when I made sex more important than she was. I was guilty for that. I was not guilty for being with her cousin. I hoped she could see in my eyes how much I cared.

Breaking the tension, Ryder walked over and teased, "What's up, dude? Ariel's asking me why you ain't called her girl back."

"What do you mean?" I asked.

He shrugged his shoulders.

"Dude, she's pissed at me. Thinks I hit on her cousin," I explained. "For real, though, I didn't know she called."

"Yeah and judging from the way she's checking you out, it looks like she wants back in. Don't blow it, Cruz," he teased.

"Cool, superstar," I pushed him and said.

"We aren't yet, but next year, boy, it's gonna be our turn for real. Scouts, look out."

Ford came over and said, "You are a superstar, Ryder. Word's out, ESPN has you ranked going into next year as a five-star recruit."

"Whatever. Don't believe the hype," Ryder said, being humble.

I was super happy for Ryder. He was trying not to make it a big deal, but it was a big deal. He had skills. Of all the high school football players out there, only a handful get that honor.

Ford leaned in and said, "And, Mr. Cruz, you are getting mad love too. I'm hearing four stars."

"From who?" I questioned, not believing that. "Not the way I played in the last game."

Ryder popped me in the chest and said, "Don't trip; you have stats: height, weight, speed, explosion, and instincts. You're good, man, and you know it."

Emerson and Stone walked over, and Emerson said, "What y'all yapping about over here?"

We filled them in on the sports talk. I also took a minute to tell them about the Bones. We all breathed a deep sigh of relief.

I noticed the girls checking us out. My boys wanted to be with them. Learning Yaris had been trying to get in touch with me made me want to get to her and clear up any misunderstanding between us.

"Go handle yo' business," Ryder said as he left to be with Ariel.

All of them disbursed and left me. It seemed like the room stood still and Yaris and I were the only ones there. She could not stop watching me. And to think she called me and I hadn't returned her call, I knew she must be going crazy.

She looked so lovely in her party dress. I knew I loved her, and she needed to know it. We were just teens, but my feelings were very, very real.

Our time for a break was over. Since I wasn't walking over to her, she turned. However, I wasn't letting her get away. I was quickly by her side. I covered her eyes, and gently kissed her. She turned, and her watery eyes told me she loved me back.

At the same time, we said, "I'm sorry."

"Please, I need to explain the way I acted after you told me you weren't pregnant," I said.

"I was stressed about the gang, so I wasn't thinking about what you'd just been through and the way you were feeling, and that was wrong. Thankfully the Bones and Loco are behind me. I want you in my life."

She smiled and said, "Really, are you sure?"

Pulling her close, I said, "Yeah, I'm sure. I was wrong to give you an ultimatum. You've been through a lot, and I added to it. Now let me be honest: I do want us to be together again, but no pressure from me anymore. I love you. I care about you. I'm glad you're not having a kid, and I want it to stay that way for quite a while. Be my girl again. Know I'll never betray you with your cousin or any other girl. You're my heart. Can you forgive me?"

She squeezed me real tight. "I love you too. I should have known you weren't pursuing Gigi. I know you care, and scaring you about being a teen father is enough to make any man run."

"You calling me a man, huh?"

She smiled, and our lips touched. "If the shoe fits. It's like you've grown up so much over the last few weeks. Let's not hurt each other anymore."

I agreed. We enjoyed the rest of the evening. My girl was my girl again.

It was Thanksgiving morning, and I had a lot to be thankful for. Everything wasn't perfect, but things were much better. I'd been through a lot over the last few weeks, and if going through obstacles had made me a better man, then I guess it was all worth it because I did learn a lot. I heard my phone vibrate, and I rolled over to get it.

It was a text from Yaris that read, "Are you coming to dinner?"

I was clueless as to what she was talking about. It was Thanksgiving. I wasn't going to leave my mom by herself.

"Nah, I don't think so," I texted back.

"My dad just said y'all were coming."

Before I could ask her to explain further, my mom knocked on my door.

"Honey, you in there?"

"Yes, ma'am."

"The Fernandezes have invited us to their house for Thanksgiving dinner. I figured you would want to go, so I accepted. That's all right, right?"

I just got up and hugged my mom real tight.

"What's this for?" she asked.

"It's Thanksgiving, and I'm thankful for you."

"I'm thankful for you too, baby. I know we've had a hard past couple of weeks, but I'm proud of you. You kept your head on straight, made the right decisions, and came through so much."

"You know Yaris thinks you don't like her."

"I have been hard on her. But I'm trying to change my ways all the way around, so it's good that we're going over there. I'll make a point to talk to her. They have such a nice family. It was so sweet of them to invite us to share the holiday with them."

I looked down. I hated that my family was all messed up. My mom was a single mother because of my deadbeat dad. He needed to get a grip. He needed to take responsibility. He needed to drop the lawsuit. I wasn't sure where we were with all of that, so I asked her.

"It's nothing I want you worrying about."

"Well, if it involves you, Mom, of course I'm going to worry."

"Well, look at you growing up," she said as she smiled wider than the state of Texas.

"Do you like it here, Mom?"

"Yes, I'm starting to make good friends, and I'm getting a promotion."

"You're already assistant manager."

"I know. They're opening up a new store, and I'm going to run it."

"No way, Mom!"

"Yes, it's true. I know I take on crazy hours, and the only reason I have a little bit of apprehension about taking the job is because the hours are going to be even worse. And with you almost halfway through your junior year, almost a senior already, I just don't know …"

"No, Mom. Don't even think about me. This is your time to shine."

"You're sure you're going to be all right?"

"You just said I'm making better decisions, Mom. We need this for our family. I just don't want Dad in your pockets."

"Well, he's supposed to be coming over here in a little while."

"What do you mean?" I said, completely upset.

"He said he wanted to come and talk to me," she explained.

"Then he should've done that over the phone."

"But it's Thanksgiving, and I'm being blessed with this job. I don't want to have a hard heart, and I don't want to keep your father away from you. He has something to say that he needs to come here and say in person."

"But, Mom, you don't know everything," I said, thinking of how my dad was the one who had really connected me with the gang because of his outstanding debt.

She shocked me when she said, "No, he's told me some of the things he's done to you."

"I bet he didn't tell you everything," I said, thinking she wouldn't let him come over if he'd told her that.

Not my mom. She didn't play. "I know about the money he borrowed."

Dumbfounded, I asked, "And is it okay with you if he comes?"

"It's okay. We got to move on from this place, Hagen. Let's get every area of our lives straight so we can move forward. No looking over our shoulders, no regret, no anger."

About an hour later our doorbell rang. I was the first one to it.

"Why are you here?" I said to my father.

"Let him in, son."

"No, Mom. The last time he was here it was crazy."

"You're right, son, to protect your mom like that, and I just came to tell you that I'm sorry and that I'm dropping my lawsuit. I want a relationship with you, Hagen. I know I messed up. I got a job in Alabama, and I'll be sending money back to your mom instead of asking her to take care of me. I plan to prove to you that I've changed."

"Fine," I said.

He waved at my mom, turned, and started walking out, but I couldn't just let him leave. He was my father. As much as thinking of him killed me, I knew letting him go this way and not really releasing all of the aches inside would be way worse. So I rushed up to him and hugged him tight. With that hug I was saying, "Please change; I believe you can. Thanks for dropping your suit, and take care."

And with him hugging me back I felt him

saying, "I will. You're going to be okay, and I'm glad you started manning up." And after that embrace, I really did feel better.

Dinner at Yaris's house was super special. The meal was fabulous, and the atmosphere was perfect. Yaris and I were back as a couple. My mom had her life going on, and Yaris's dad seemed happy that his restaurant was headed in the right direction. Thanks to all our help and his restaurant being that good in the first place, more people were uncovering the hidden gem.

After dinner Gigi came over to us and said, "Yaris, do you mind if I talk to Hagen for a second?"

Yaris said, "No problem." She gave me a kiss on the cheek and walked away. I honestly didn't want to be alone with her cousin. I know all hearts and minds were cleared, but mine needed to keep her at arm's length because my heart was really for her cousin, and I didn't have time for any foolishness.

"I just wanted to say ..." she stepped closer, and I put my arm out.

"That's close enough."

"I know you don't trust me."

"No, I don't."

"I just wanted to say I apologize for what happened, and I'm really excited you and Yaris worked everything out."

"Okay, cool."

"But can we at least be friends?" she said before I could get away. "I mean, I'm new here, and I don't know anybody."

I wanted to tell her, "Get out of my face and don't ever speak to me again." But that wasn't the gentlemanly thing to do. Knowing that we all need a second chance at some point, I said, "Sure."

She smiled.

Quickly I went to go find Yaris, but I was stopped dead in my tracks when I heard her and my mom having a discussion.

"I just wanted to apologize to you, Yaris. You know Hagen's my son, my only child, and I'm protective of him. I know he's growing up, and I've got to let go of the reins. I just didn't want you and him making any of the mistakes I made, but I think you're a precious girl, and I shouldn't have made you feel otherwise. Will you forgive me?"

"Yes, ma'am," Yaris said as she gave my mom a hug.

My mom spotted me and said, "I think he wants a hug too." And I went over and hugged both of the special women in my life.

A while later I passed George in the hallway.

"Hey, man," he said glumly.

I stopped him and asked, "You all right? You good?"

"Yeah, I just don't wish ill on no one, and part of me hates that Loco's in jail ..."

I raised my eyebrows at him like, *Are you kidding me?* George nodded and said, "But he made his own bed. When you try to live the fast life it isn't too pretty when you get slowed down. You're doing the right thing. Stay in school, keep working on your game, and have the right kind of dreams."

"That's what's up," I told him as I gave him dap.

The night ended better than it started. My mom let me take Yaris to the movies after I took her back home. We met up with our friends. Ford and Skylar were still going strong. Ryder was trying to act cool, but I could tell he was into Ariel. Emerson and Vanessa didn't care that the world knew they were into each other, and Stone and Victoria were hand in hand.

A lot of guys try to be players. I thought we were lucky to have girls who cared about us and friendships that were real. When I needed them, they had my back. When I didn't play my best game, they didn't blame me. When I was happy, they were happy for me. I knew life wasn't going to be perfect all the time and that trouble might even be lurking around the bend. But I also knew that the next time I faced adversity, I wasn't going to punk out and dodge it. Nah, I learned how to be a man and stand tall, make great choices, work hard, forgive myself when I messed up, and strive to be better than I was yesterday. If I could do all that, I'd truly be a man.

I leaned over in my seat and kissed my girl before the movie started. Seeing my friends happy with their dates too, I smiled and knew we'd get to the Dome next football season. My dad was on the right track, my mom was getting a promotion, Loco was taken care of, and I would keep working on my grades to secure a bright future for myself. It feels good when it all works.

STEPHANIE PERRY MOORE is the author of many YA inspirational fiction titles, including the *Lockwood Lions* series, the *Payton Skky* series, the *Laurel Shadrach* series, the *Perry Skky Jr.* series, the *Yasmin Peace* series, the *Faith Thomas Novelzine* series, the *Carmen Browne* series, the *Morgan Love* series, and the *Beta Gamma Pi* series. Mrs. Moore speaks with young people across the country, encouraging them to achieve every attainable dream. She currently lives in the greater Atlanta area with her husband, Derrick, and their three children. Visit her website at www.stephanieperrymoore.com.

DERRICK MOORE is a former NFL running back and currently the developmental coach for the Georgia Institute of Technology. He is also the author of *The Great Adventure* and *It's Possible: Turning Your Dreams into Reality*. Mr. Moore is a motivational speaker and shares with audiences everywhere how to climb the mountain in their lives and not stop until they have reached the top. He and his wife, Stephanie, have co-authored the *Alec London* series. Visit his website at www.derrickmoorespeaking.com.

WANT A DIFFERENT
point of view?

JUST *flip* THE BOOK!

WANT A DIFFERENT
point of view?

JUST *flip* THE BOOK!

STEPHANIE PERRY MOORE is the author of many YA inspirational fiction titles, including the *Lockwood Lions* series, the *Payton Skky* series, the *Laurel Shadrach* series, the *Perry Skky Jr.* series, the *Yasmin Peace* series, the *Faith Thomas Novelzine* series, the *Carmen Browne* series, the *Morgan Love* series, and the *Beta Gamma Pi* series. Mrs. Moore speaks with young people across the country, encouraging them to achieve every attainable dream. She currently lives in the greater Atlanta area with her husband, Derrick, and their three children. Visit her website at www. stephanieperrymoore.com.